Also by the same author
The rape of Bhudevi.

Forthcoming books:
Arabian Sadiqui Nights.

PTA-44

iAnand

PARTRIDGE
A Penguin Random House Company

To order additional copies of this book, contact
Partridge India
000 800 10062 62
www.partridgepublishing.com/india
orders.india@partridgepublishing.com

ACKNOWLEDGEMENT

At first I must thank fellow travelers of the 6:08 and 7:11 PM Shivaji Nagar to Lonavala local train and fellow travelers in the Indrayani express going from Lonavala to Shivaji Nagar at 8:02 AM, who patiently accepted the author feverishly typing on his mobile, while the train swayed and moved on with the Author often, accidentally falling on them or stepping on their shoes!

Thanks to Jim Cahill, Chief Blogger, Surface Dweller, and Head of Social Media for Emerson Process Management.

To, Raji

CONTENTS

BOOK ONE

BOOK TWO

LIST OF MAIN CHARACTERS:

Mani: The AVP of Building One.

Malar: Mani's Wife.

Andy: DCS engineer in Building One.

Jay: DCS Engineer and Andy's friend.

Aarti: Andy's love.

Kiran: Aarti's Brother.

Bhiku Patil: Aarti's Cousin.

Srinivas: General Manager in Building One

Ramesh: General Manager in Building One

Subba: Manager Operator Training Simulator

Cahill: Senior Manager at supplier company USA

Jerry: Senior Manager at supplier company USA.

Paresh: Manager at Indian operations of Supplier company

Malathy: Srinivas's Wife.

BOOK ONE

Not a place for the flamboyant!

"What are you doing here?"

"What do you mean by that?"

"I mean, your flamboyant style, 'I don't give a shit about you' way of talking . . . . You know what I mean. This place, this 'field' of yours, has always been for the subdued." Ramesh was a chemical engineer and Andy an Instrument Engineer. Instrument Engineer's provided instrument and control services in the petrochemical industry that they were in.

"Awww C'mon, who cares? We are all the cogs of a wheel or links in a chain or whatever . . . My opinion is as important as anyone else's, and, just a little bit more . . .

(couple of winks) . . . See being Instru and control, gives me an edge over you guys. Ha ha . . ."

'Instru' is a colloquial for Instrumentation.

"I mean all the Instru guys I have met, they are subdued. They understand that they are secondary citizens. This world always belonged to the chemical engineers. Even the top boss is from UDCT. You guys just serve a purpose. We always ruled the roost . . . . so to speak. Instru guys always have to answer first . . . for all failures."

UDCT is University Department of Chemical Technology, a premier chemical engineering institute in Munbai, India.

"That was the past. When you had petrochemical plants and control rooms tied to that plant.

Now, that's not the case. You could produce anywhere and control from anywhere. If you become too 'snooty', and 'Zatak' . . . We move the stuff from here . . ."

"What's this 'Zatak'?

"That's the new-style sound. You guys always teased me about the different sound's that I make when I speak and well . . . this is the latest now . . . Learn something from me . . . 'Zatak'."

Andy's speech had been colorful in the past. He always used to use sounds like "zapak se", "chiding", "dhan-ta-dan" . . . Of course, there is a popular song on this "Dhan-ta-dan" sound in a movie "Kaminey."

However, Andy was trying to leave that behind now. He used such sounds quite rarely.

"Bhai (brother), you are not Tom Cruise in Mission Impossible, Frankly, you are not even Ving Rhames or the other guy who helps Ethan Hunt, you are more like the character who appears for a few seconds in a movie . . . Anyway, you would have learnt this 'Zatak' from that chick from Airoli."

"Which chick? Any ways boss, your concept is like old times. . . . We are like James Bond, we do everything ourselves. All others do not matter . . ."(Now striking a James Bond shooting a gun pose)

"Ha Ha . . . So Miss Airoli, . . . is like one of the chicks that comes in the movie but don't matter . . ."

"What, Airoli Chick???"

"You mean 'Which' Airoli chick . . . or 'Airoli chick? Who?' . . . You think I do not know. You have abandoned the whole group, and you have started coming in the 'cut bogie' . . . You rush to the side that opens to the ladies first class and this girl gets in at Airoli and you pass some chits and messages in the train . . . 'Hamare jasoos charron aur phaile huyen hain' (our spies are spread over everywhere) . . ."

A 'cut bogie' is colloquial for a train compartment that houses a gents compartment on one side and ladies on the other side, with a partition through which you can see the other side.

"She is just a friend."

"Saale! As if I don't know about you." (Saale literally means Brother-in-law, but is used to show various emotions from mild aggression to exasperation to anything that you can think of . . .)

"Nahin, (no) . . . . There is nothing like that" (going on).

"See, why do you think you are getting late every evening? Missing the 6:30 local . . . hunh . . . You introduce her to the group . . . I mean . . . properly . . . and see what wonders can happen . . . get my drift . . . You may be the expert in the systems, but we still rule the roost . . ."

"Harami! You guys have been doing this willfully . . . I was wondering, why at least one of you has some problem cropping up late in the evening. I should have known . . ."

"Ha ha . . . you think that you still have something in PTA plant, that you can teach us. Man, we were literally born in PTA plant. My father was an operator in Patalganga. I have been there as a child during open house and festivals . . . when the management would allow the families to visit. I was one of the first operators when the control room was moved to Ghansoli."

"All this shifting of control rooms is possible only because of instrument and control technology. Without automation where would all this business be? We are now controlling 43 PTA plants from across the globe from one place in Ghansoli. Can you imagine that happening . . . with 'just' chemical engineering?" Many Indian's use 'Just' to mean 'only'.

"Okay . . . let's park it for now (you big or me big thing) . . . Do you think Marshall Cahill will be able to fix this issue with the feed mix Automator, for the project 'PTA44' in time . . . I heard that we would be delayed."

"Should be (able to) . . . Okay . . . Finish your coffee fast, I have to go."

"Hey no, you go ahead. I will control with my mobile workstation for some time.

I am waiting for Subba. We have to discuss a few things. And hey, there are issues with the training module. I'll try to find out how major the issue is . . . . We will see that in the afternoon."

"Ciao . . . I have to 'initiate' a bunch of trainees coming in tomorrow. I have to practice."

"Young crowd . . . Watch out . . . Don't start chasing some young trainee and ditch miss Airoli . . . Ha Ha . . ."

"C'ya Ramesh . . . ."

"Well, welcome to our organization. I'll briefly explain you the history of this place. Where you are standing today, these glass lined towers, buildings with central A/C . . . well . . . these were not here a few years ago . . ."

"Andy, don't do a 'James Michener' on Ghansoli . . ."

"C'mon Jay, let me practice . . ."

"These youngsters are Instrument and Control Engineers with some experience. You can start directly with the systems that we have."

"Jay, you are so devoid of any romance, any color . . . . You need to start with something that is not Instrumentation and control . . ."

"I was thinking that you'd start with ancient dinosaur birds that roamed these lands, then go to 'aadi manav'(pre-humans), then the history attached to Ramayana and some things from Mahabharata and later day kings, Shivaji Maharaj's rule to Britishers and, then to Thane-Belapur industrial belt, then Nilon Petrochem plant here and then the takeover and decommissioning of the old plant and establishment of the new city and EPC offices here . . . It's an hour's introduction and not a four day history lesson . . . ha ha . . ."

"You will remain a "Ghonchu" . . . . Let me practice my routine . . ." Again, you cannot think of any meaning to Ghonchu . . . except maybe an 'Idiot' or an 'irritating person'. Often the word 'Ghonchu' is attributed to a film star 'Shatrughan Sinha' whose daughter Sonakshi is a popular heroine now-a-days.

"You are too much . . . I've never seen such a flamboyant Instru guy . . . Generally we are a very subdued, conservative community . . ."

"This is the second time I've heard that today . . . I am what I am . . ."

"What's with the Airoli girl?"

"What Airoli girl?"

"Hamare Jasoos charo aur faile huwe hain . . . ." (our spies are spread over everywhere)

"Déjà vu . . . Again the same dialogue . . ."

"Who else?"

"Ramesh . . . He was giving the same crap about me being too outgoing."

"You seem to get into trouble with your extrovert style. You want to rise too fast."

"So what's wrong with that? I feel confident of the things that I do."

"Everybody appreciates you in your face, but many are likely to be finding your success difficult to digest. And I think that the management would use you to make this PTA44 successful. However, any glitch and then you will land up in all kinds of trouble. You will be the fall guy . . . Watch out!"

"You fret too much. You have to accept your karma. Do your task and leave it to god."

"That's easy to hear in a 'Pravachan' (religious sermon), but not when something bad happens to you along the way. Look, I'm telling you all this because, we were in college together. The rest is your decision . . ."

"Ok. I'll lay low for some time."

"No you won't. You'll say this and Mani would come along and take a commitment from you, shift the dates ahead by a few days, and you will hang upon his words and commit. I know you. They'll throw a challenge in your face, and you'll say 'yes'."

"I'll be careful and not let that happen" (in the future).

"Anyway, what's with this Airoli chick?"

"Nothing so far. We are 'just friends'."

"Watch out. That girl looks a beautiful Maharashtrian."

"What such white skin, almost milky white, her features are almost Gujju. I believe that she'll be a Gujju Patel like me."

Maharashtrians are Indians living in Maharashtra, a state in India and generally speak Marathi. While 'Gujju' or Gujarathi's are people from the Gujarath state, now well known all over the world due to their Chief Minister, Narendra Modi.

"I think she looks more local . . . She is a 'Gori' (white colored girl) by Indian standards, for actual white you need to see the Europeans . . . . Be careful, some of these local girls have relatives who are goons and into politics and things like that. Things could get very ugly if they turn out that kind."

"There is nothing like that going on. Don't worry. Let me focus on my work."

"And since when have you stopped at 'Just Being Friends'"

———⚜———

"The training module is not working."

"Ramesh, what do you mean by not working?"

"I had my team run it today, and they told me that it was not working."

"We had tested it thoroughly in USA, and everything was perfect. I see no reason why it should not be working."

"I called Subba and he informed me that nothing is working. What did you guys do in USA? You spent time in 'Baywatch'? Subba told me that you guys spent a lot on dance bars?"

"Kuch bhi kya!! (colloquial Hindi for nonsense)". Andy said. He thought, Subba must be bugged because he did not get to go. "First Austin is far away from sea beaches, and you are likely to see more bikini-clad girls in Goa rather than Houston. This whole thing about 'USA and Baywatch' is such crap and in bad spirits. I have seen those guys come in at 3:00AM at times and work hard until 6 in the evening. And when they work, they work. So, they like their weekends, so what?"

"I heard you guys spent all your money in dance bars."

"You mean 'strip tease joints'. They have a few bars like that. They dragged me once to it. I did not enjoy it that much."

———

"Subba's friend was in Houston and gave him a graphic description. It seems like a lot of fun."

Dance bars were a typical Mumbai phenomenon of the 1990's. Banned for a long time and then permitted to reopen. A den of vices. Andy had a very low opinion of the dance bars and the people who went there. Everyone knew that he did not go to any such joints.

"Chodo naa (leave it be). What we were discussing was the training module."

"Yes sir!" Some Sarcasm in his voice, "Nothing is working. And everybody suspects that the three of you 'just—chilled' for a month and half, and the entire SOS thing and late-night meetings were a sham. In fact, Srinivas seems to have boasted that he took a call from a dance bar once. Everybody is laughing with him and at the same time, reporting on him when he turns his back. Things are not looking good."

"Nothing could be farther from the truth."

Andy had worked conscientiously, and he was sure that nothing was wrong with the training module. He had himself done each test meticulously. He had spent days and evenings and some nights, in the testing room, checking each scenario, each safety measure and nothing could have gone wrong.

Subba dropped in. The moment he saw Andy, he started singing a Hindi song . . 'Just-Chill . . . Chill . . . Chill' which had been a popular Hindi Song in its days . . .

"So the cool people are here." He said sarcastically, now directly looking at Andy. "Or should I say 'chilled' people".

"Hey Subba! Take it easy." Ramesh chipped in.

"What 'take it easy'! f#$%&#g s##t. it was my weekly off today, and I was to go to Lonavala. But here I am . . . . In the OTS room! Wasting a whole day before I realized that these guys had 'Just-chilled' in USA. And nothing was working." Some of the Indian slurs and swearing in English use adjectives that contort the literal meaning of the words such spoken!

"Mind your language Subba! Your accusation is incorrect."

Subba cooled a little, but was still visibly angry "What mind my language . . . . You guys have wasted company time and money, and I have to keep quiet and waste all my leave's working in the office. Up yours . . . ."

Andy felt his BP rise, but before he could snap at Subba, Ramesh interjected.

"We will get to the bottom of this Subba. Meanwhile let us keep our tempers low and do some fact finding here."

Everyone was quiet. Andy knew where this was leading to. Ramesh wanted some news or some accusation against Srinivas.

"I'm sorry Andy," Subba apologized. "But, it is very frustrating. After working so hard in this project, I have felt left out of the key processes and in my area of expertise. And to top that, now I am left with 'crap' that is not working and am 'pissed'. The entire company' s investment in this is wasted. And we will get bad points in our increment and appraisals due to this."

Subba had been keen on being in Austin for the OTS tests, but the management had sent Singh, who was relatively new and Singh would have learnt about the software rather than be able to contribute to it.

"Can you tell me what is wrong?" Andy asked again.

Ramesh cut this and said, "That's ok Andy . . . What is wrong can wait. I want to know, how you guys spent your time there. How could things have goofed up like this, with so many extensions to the whole things and additional budgets being sanctioned and what not? Management is going to be very-very upset with the way things have turned out."

"Hey Ramesh, I was in the office most of the time. I did not even do any trips in USA. So this is ridiculous! Leave all this gossip and jokes aside and just tell me what is wrong, and I will fix it."

Andy knew that the decision by Mani to send Srinivas instead of Ramesh irked many. Subba's trip was canceled due to budget limitations. So he was pissed.

All said and done, Subba was not one to report anything incorrectly. He had seen a few such 'misfortunes' come his way during his stint in this company, but he was always shown the next 'carrot', and he would get workaholic soon . . .

Andy did not want to be a part of the showdown between Srinivas and Ramesh. As they say, never stand behind an ass and be ahead of a boss. Either way, you will get kicked.

"See Ramesh, I can only tell you of when Srinivas was with me . . . . what he did then. His agenda and things he was to do as told by management to him, is beyond my jurisdiction."

"Andy, you are becoming smarter by the day . . . Watch out, but supporting Srinivas will not get you anywhere." Obviously, Ramesh felt annoyed with Andy.

"Ramesh, let's not waste time. I am not against you or anyone. You know Srinivas and I know Srinivas. Frankly, when he was not there, I was happy that he was not there to bother me when I was working . . . . Otherwise, nothing would have happened in another six months." Andy did not add that though Srinivas seemed a buffoon and one who could achieve little, he had given all the pointers to fix the bugs and demanded so many tests that showed his depth of knowledge in PTA process operations.

"Ha ha ha. What you say is true." Ramesh gave up. He knew that Andy would not be the one to 'tell-on' others. However, these few words against his colleague Srinivas put some warmth in him. "Subba, give the details of the issues."

"What details boss . . . everything is like as it was six months ago. I mean that everything is like PTA12. The startup programs, the whole process, and the tags, and everything . . . everything. Only the software's title is PTA44. It is a joke, except that it is not funny."

"Hah! We have loaded the wrong file. We should have loaded the latest file from the backup taken after testing in Austin. Ramesh, I gave you the copy last week. That is the latest software."

Ramesh "OK. Let me check on this and get back to you."

Marshall Cahill of the Wild West

—◆—

66**T**his is no longer a monopoly business. When the CEO started out in this business, nobody believed us. We moved into uncharted waters. We had PTA plant experience in several continents. We were the pioneers in this 'transition'. We had the advantages of being the first movers.

We could demand a premium in the market. Our experience removed the risk from others who were operating their plant in an inefficient way.

However, now the traditional Indian IT service providers have entered the fray . . . . We have to operate with small margins. Even when the clients know that we are the best place to come for PTA operations, they would use the BFSI majors to bring down the price.

The company depends on you to provide the PTA44 transition 'on—time' and 'very-smooth'. You know how 'jittery' these new companies are handing over their plant operations to us.

Am I clear?"

Silence for a few seconds:

"Yes Sir."

"Good Andy, I rely on you to do the excellent work as always. The RFAT (Remote-Operations Factory Acceptance Tests) has been delayed, and their operations team has not approved the reactor startup so far. Why this delay?"

"They had certain . . . hmmnn . . . 'quirky' requirements with their startup logic. We explained our experience in this. But they would not budge. Especially their Steven was not convinced. But now things have been sort of 'ironed out'. We got delayed because of their stubborn refusal to listen to us on the startup program. Finally, we had to do it their way."

"I know that this must have been frustrating for all of you, but we have to be careful with this 'party'(company). They are very difficult. Their management is with us, but most of the staff has been very reluctant. We get flogged from all sides on this . . . .

Their management and ours will be after us if there is any delay. Already they are asking for a few heads to roll because of these few days that we are behind schedule. It is with much difficulty that I have retained the team. We need to move this thing ahead."

"Ok Sir."

"We need to move this Feed mix thing Andy. What's the status? Did you check with Marshall Cahill?"

"Will do that . . ."

"Andy, you need to be more proactive. Check with him. You never know with Americans . . . They could be in some vacation and nobody in office to work for a week or so. Or he could be 'Chilling' in some beach like in 'Baywatch' . . ."

"Haha . . . (everybody laughing)"

The use of the words 'Chilling' and 'Baywatch' troubled Andy. It looked like some storm was brewing, and he needed to watch out.

"They are all cowboys. This Marshall Cahill of yours is very intelligent, but with Americans, you have to have constant follow-up . . . . Else, he will be gone to some 'rodeo show' or 'strawberry festival' or to Las Vegas strip, and before you know, times up! And your feedmix system would be never coming up . . ."

"No Sir, Cahill was in office entire last week, working more than 12 hours a week on the feed mix system. He is different. You see the old plant had so little system that the people used any feed mix pattern . . ."

"No wonder they had so many issues. Hope you did not give him our feed mix recipe and algorithm."?

"No Sir. We have just given him the algorithm and some random values. They cannot use this on any feed-mix system. Only the weighing of the individual powders and liquids will be tested. Even the client will not know."

"Good! Check with Marshall Cahill and find out what's going on with the feed mix system."?

Ramesh:" Marshall Cahill! Kem Cho (how are you Marshall Cahill)?"

Cahill : "(accented) Maja Ma (enjoying) . . ."

Ramesh: "I thought you were working all of last week and weekend."

Cahill: "Yes, I meant enjoying the pain."

Andy: "He had to work all the weekend. And the processes in his company do not allow them to work during the weekends. So it was a big task for Marshall."

Ramesh: "Here, you do not have to seek permission to work on any day, but you have to explain when you do not work on a weekend . . . Ha Ha . . ."

"Ha Ha . . ."

Ramesh: "Chalo, I'll leave for now as I have to go to another meeting. Andy will continue. Please do not forget to record the conference call notes and also circulate to our boss Mani."

"C'ya."

Ramesh: "Bye and good morning . . ."

"So, let's get down to business Marshall."

"Andy, no breakthrough yet. The standard solution does not work. We tried to shift the whole system design to the left as per our last conversation, but even that will not work."

"Why?"

"They have two 'unrecorded' beams on the left side."

"What do you mean by 'unrecorded beams'?"

"This old plant, the guys would do whatever field modifications they could think of, any time they wanted to, and not put anything on their drawings. So we have all the old plant drawings, and these have so many things that are not recorded, that we end up facing all these difficulties."

"But didn't your company send a team for the site visit? They should have recorded this."

"Yes a Pune team had gone on the site visit."

"Then this is their fault, and they should answer and provide a final design."

"Let me see if I can get someone from the Pune team on-line for the same. Let's convene again after 15 minutes."

"OK" (phones hang up).

⚜

"What's this 'Marshall Cahill' business?"

"That's a long story. These guys had come to USA some five years back. And they were staying in Houston, and I went there to discuss the design of the feed mix system.

(at that time) This was a recent innovation that we had done in those days. These guys wanted to know all the technical details. The logic, the mechanisms, the works . . .

No answers were given for the first few days except the specifications, and once the confidentiality agreement was signed; I was called in.

Meanwhile, their boss . . . Mani had seen 'US Marshall Cahill' on TV in the hotel and when I arrived there and introduced myself, he went "Ah like Marshall Cahill." And the name was used in a jovial way. Somehow, the name stuck . . ."

"So what are the issues? I got a call from the group president this morning asking me to look over this issue.

Which means that he (group president) got it from somewhere high up in India."

"(phone rings) Looks like Paresh is now online."

"Hi Paresh."

"Hi Marshall."

"Even our guys!!!" (Jerry chuckles)

"It has spread like a virus Jerry."

"Oh! The Virus started in Akola and has now spread to Pune. Six people have died so far." Paresh, misunderstanding for a Virus scare in India.

"What Virus?"

"The H23N44 Virus. It has been all over the news. In fact, we have a three-day holiday next week while the local administration urges all to get an antidote shot?

But I doubt if everyone will get a shot. Most people here believe that like all flu, this has a three day period, in which you will develop immunity and its spread will be arrested."

"No Paresh, we were not talking about the H23N44 virus."

"Then what other virus, Marshall?"

"Nothing . . . Don't worry . . . just small talk here."

"OK."

"Anyway Paresh, we are getting blasted here by the PTA44 client. We had gone on a site visit, and they want to know, why we did not capture all the details during the visit."

"Marshall, Jerry, I do not know what to say now . . . First they gave us visa after two months delay. Then, there was the terrorist incident in that country and all travel was restricted. Then we went to the plant, and the local staff had not made the site pass arrangements.

Our personnel then went through three days of fire and safety training, before they could enter the plant.

And when they did, there were no drawings!

They could not take any pictures of the site! They had to make hand-sketches of the feed mix vessel and the location of the feed manhole at the top. If they had the drawings in the first place, they would have marked up the beams."

"Paresh, these beams should have come up in the drawings or hand sketches. First, we missed the wall on the right side that made us shift the orientation to the left and now this."

"Jerry, our scope was very clear. We would markup on the drawings, and the PTA44 plant people were supposed to provide us the same, BEFORE . . . Before . . . we reached the site. Nothing like this happened. In fact, the young chaps we sent were more proactive to make these drawings. We need to appreciate their efforts." Paresh wanted Marshall and Jerry to know that the arrangements were not proper. The engineers from Pune, had actually done more than was expected. Sometimes, when you are proactive, you actually get into more trouble. Had the guys returned and said that they were not provided with the drawings, then the fingers would have pointed at the end customer!

"Paresh, At this point it does not look good. This explanation of yours would seem an excuse when the top management meets next week. We have to firm up the design and provide the same to our Korean fabricator. And it looks like we do not have a start date for that, and in fact, we are three weeks from delivery."

"Jerry, the plant people (people on the plant site) were very uncooperative. Our guys had to stand there and use some napkins to make the drawings. These were then translated to white paper in their hotel. It is really a miracle that our guys used their presence of mind to come up with these sketches"

Marshall "Ok guys, we have little time right now to discuss past issues, as we have to call the PTA44 team in New Bombay. So what we say is that the drawings were not provided to us at the time of the site visit. Let me dial Andy in."?

Cahill: "Hi There Andy."

Andy: "Hi Marshall.

Cahill: "Andy, we have Paresh from Pune on line."

Paresh: "Hi Andy. How are you? When are you coming to Pune?"

Andy: "Not so well guys. What are these issues coming up at the last moment? I had a high opinion of your engineering capabilities. I did not expect you guys to be stuck for such a long time! I'm getting heat from all sides now."

Paresh: "Andy, I am sorry to be saying this, but the issues have not been made by us."

Andy: "Paresh, all these are excuses. We had to go through so much to get visas for your team.

The entire visit was not budgeted in the first place! That came up due to a small fine print in the contract, and we supported you.

Now it seems that the visit was a waste, and nothing was achieved! Now don't just say that it was not your fault but give us the solution."

Cahill: "Andy, there is so much you can predict on the outcome of the things we plan. The visit had its series of misfortunes right from the beginning."

Andy: "Well, to us, we did all that was needed to be done. We sent you guys on the 'trip'.', You came up with the preliminary drawing.

Missed out the wall on the right side and the fouling that would have happened. Your guys must have been blind to have missed that big wall on the right. And now the beams on the left. C'mon, put yourselves in my shoes for a moment and think . . . what am I supposed to tell my management?" Andy wanted to sound tough. He had heard that he was soft on vendors and quickly saw their problems. Everyone in his organization was saying that he should be tough on vendors.

Cahill: "The dimensions of the feed mix Automator were clearly explained to you. And we are clear that such a space is required for the Automator."

Andy:" Does that mean that the Automator cannot be fitted in that space?"

Cahill: "Not unless the beams on the left are cut."

Andy: "That is beyond our scope. I do not see that happening. When I recommended you for this task, I was thinking of showing my management some miraculous ways of working and getting an early promotion. Now I am looking forward to saving my job, and that would be a miracle. Guy's we need to come up with something better than that."

Cahill: "All I can say is that the standard Automator would not fit into that space."

Andy: "Why not modify the design slightly to reduce the space."

Cahill: "As of now we do not have any alternate designs. And we have a three-week deadline. That leaves us just enough space to complete the fabrication the standard unit and test it. And that too at a very fast track basis."

Andy: "Oh Shit! This whole project is going to face a big problem. The client has four more such units, and they would hold on to future orders! This is a really big problem. I don't know guys. Come up with a new solution or I don't know . . ."

(Hangs up). Andy felt that his hanging up would convey the seriousness of the issues confronting them.

"How did it go?"

"It couldn't be worse Jay. I think I have hit the bottom. My mother says that my 'saade saati' is going on" (Saade-Saati, a seven and half year cycle of misfortune as per Hindu beliefs).

"Do you know Bhiku Patil?"

"No. Who is he?"

"He is Aarti's cousin brother. Ass hole!! You wrote a love letter to this girl . . . and . . . she confided to her cousin sister . . . and sister tells brother. They get hold of the letter, and you are in very big trouble."

"Hnnh!"

"Don't look like you have been hit by a thunderbolt. What have you been up-to with this girl?"

"Hnnh!"

"Hey Andy speak up. I need to know what you are up to, because I told this guy something's and if I am wrong, then I need to look for another job somewhere far away from here. And you have kept this hidden from me for all this time. I am deeply hurt. I always thought that we were friends and now . . . with this . . . I do not know what you are doing."

"Aarti and I have been in love for almost a year now."

"What! And you have been lying to me and hiding this for a year! Man, I thought we were friends"

"I'm sorry, but I thought you guys would make fun of this, and was waiting for something to happen before confirming. Yes . . . . I told my family a few months ago. They are not happy.

The girl being Marathi. I told them that she was a 'Lewa Patel', and since the 'Lewa Patels' came to Maharashtra, they became known as Patils here. Basically they are Gujarathis. My family . . . they are ok now. They have met Aarti some time back."

"Ok Man . . . I did not expect this . . . We were from the same college, and I expected to know much before this . . . I always thought we were friends . . .

OK . . . if your family knows . . . That's good. But it seems that the girl's family does not know. The cousin here seems to be high up in the politics here. He was threatening about breaking your legs, etc etc. I told him that you two were friends . . . Just friends . . . . . You be careful when you go out tonight . . . on second thoughts, Let's go together. And if you get to get out of this affair, wear your chastity lock as far as local girls are concerned. And believe me, you do not want to be mixed up with this lot. They could be big trouble for you and your career."

Andy knew that his 'hiding stuff' from Jay would seem to be a betrayal to Jay. Jay was very magnanimous kind of guy. A guy with a big heart . . .

He was touched by Jay's gesture of going with him when he expected some trouble.

"I don't know. I need to inform Mani about the call with Marshall."

"He's left for the day. It's almost 7:00 PM. Send him a memo. He'll see it later tonight. Bad night for him and for you."

"OK. Give me a few minutes."

Jay found it very difficult to believe that Andy could be serious about any girl. Andy had been a rash, dare devil in his college days and most girls could not resist Andy.

In that remote town, where the government had built a premium engineering college, people were ultra conservative. Girls had to marry as per their family's wishes, and they had to keep their treasured 'virginity' until marriage.

However, affairs did happen and there were many bloody fights over girls. Boys who were tangled with some girl and things went wrong, found themselves with broken bones, fractures and stitches. There were many 'Khap panchayats' or vigilante groups that would beat any guy up to keep the town's moral code.

In this scenario, handsome Andy could draw out girls to meetings in gardens, where he did a lot of necking behind bushes. His escapades were discussed, 'awed at' and became legendary in their college. Boy's coming to that college from different corners of India had heard the horror stories of guys beaten up so bad, that they had to miss a couple of semesters of education.

Further, in all such cases, the teaching and administrative staffs were more sympathetic to the locals, as they themselves had become locals.

After some time, girls found out that it was safe to do some necking with Andy, as he had become so disreputable that no one would find any fault with the girl. Parents in the neighborhood were 'wary' when Andy was around.

But yet Andy found out a way to befriend and do things to girls that the whole teenage lot of the college wanted to, but did not have the guts.

And as his 'repute' or 'disrepute' grew, Andy would do almost anything to get a date and do some necking. He had jumped fences and walked to the girl's window and talked with them, sweet nothings, late in the evening. He had arrived early behind the milkman or newspaper vendor and got an early-morning kiss. Every few days, he seemed to be discovering a new way of doing the same-old things.

Girls would somehow rush out with the lamest of excuses and get a kiss or two, hidden from their parent's sight . . . The thrill and the adrenalin rush that was there in those scenes, with parents in close proximity and doing what was forbidden, can only be experienced.

Andy at times vividly described, to his close circle, all the touching and necking that he did. To the sex-starved teenagers, he was a hero, who some envied, some were plainly jealous of him and some hoped that he should get bashed and end up with stitches. However, those predictions and wishes never materialized. Andy was very-very lucky indeed.

Many girls found crossing that thin line of honor difficult. They even thought kissing and necking as mortal sins. But Andy always promised them that eventually they would get married, so all this was justified.

By the third year of engineering, Andy had promised marriage to 18 girls. Jay always felt that Andy stopped at necking because the girls were wary of his reputation. Though Jay never had guts to cross the line, his analysis was that Andy would score more, if he did not promise marriage earlier to get into necking, but extract going all the way before he promised.

He had theoretically argued with Andy many a times to hold on to the promises for some time longer. But when the moment came, Andy just slipped and promised whatever was needed to go one step ahead.

Andy had a lot of guts. And he was kind of a 'hero' with the guys in college. While many were tongue tied and shy in matters related to girls, Andy was very bold.

Jay remembered a time in Dassera, when they had gone to Vadodra on a college sponsored industry visit. Andy was the Class Representative, and hence he had the college's SLR camera. They had found a ground where there was a 'Garba Dance' event organized.

First, he impressed the security guard that he was from Bollywood, and come on a talent scout. His smooth talking and a 50 rupee note that he borrowed from Manish, got them in. Then he went very close, to the girls dancing on the ground. Areas, where only those in Garba attire could be allowed.

Then, he picked the most beautiful girl on the Garba ground. He took several pictures and Jay did not know what magic he weaved, but soon he had the girl talking with him in between the dances.

Between dances, Andy told the girl that she had a promising future in Bollywood, but that Vadodra had girls who though beautiful, did not stand a chance against Bombay girls due to less skin exposure. He almost got the girl to believe that they should together somehow defeat the Bombay girls.

Within 10 minutes, the girl was convinced that she had to do something for Vadodra. In fact, she desired to show them Bombay girls what Vadodra had!

And a few minutes later, he had lured the girl between some parked cars and she had asked him to help her remove her bra and he asked her to open some cleavage. He even helped her do that. Jay and a few from Andy's chosen close circle of friends had actually seen everything, hidden from the 'Garba Gori's' view. They had seen him fondle her and kiss her hungrily even as he helped her do the bold act.

He also did some necking with the girl in the parking lot. He took her address, promised her eternal love and companionship. Jay had seriously felt that Andy was finally hooked.

The girl was beautiful. And for the next half hour, Andy got her to do some very sexy moves and had several trips to the parking lot. He seemed totally intoxicated by her. Andy would be bent over, his body at very different awkward angles, which impressed the girls that he was a real pro. But finally, the pictures did not turn out very good, because Andy was not a good photographer.

Next day they were to go back to their college town. In the train journey, he only talked about the Garba girl. And Jay felt he had seen Andy fall in love.

The day following the train journey, they were back in town, and Andy was with other girls and dates. He never wrote to the Garba girl. The 'Garba gori' had been a discussion in college for a few days and though Andy did not know, this event had raised the feeling of awe, a notch higher, in students who held him in awe. To those who had considered him a 'hero' until then, he had become a 'super hero', and those who had disliked him so far now hated him even more.

Jay thought that Andy was unscrupulous to the core while Andy was just living his teenage life. He was exploring his new-found freedom and was not aware of the collateral damage that his actions were causing.

Jay felt that Andy could not be serious about Aarti.

No way!

Andy was not a lesser mortal to give up his flamboyant life and toil 9-5 for a single woman.

Andy would end up a bachelor with several girls in his life, and maybe illicitly father some children. Well, that's what everyone in college had thought.

However, Andy had changed.

When Jay had seen Andy a few years later, he could barely recognize the characteristics. Andy worked 10-12 hours a day, and was depended upon to deliver results. There was a seriousness about him that had not been evident in the past. Had Andy matured and come to the 'boring' world of ordinary people?

So could Andy be serious about Aarti?

Jay was unsure.

He had seen an Andy, to whom tomorrow meant nothing. Tomorrow probably never existed to that Andy!

And now he had visibly changed. Maybe he had matured.

Jay's mind had been caught in these two opposite thoughts for some time, and he could not make up his mind. Let things take their own course . . . Why judge?

"Let's leave."

AAWAJ KUNACHA?

Andy surmised that he was in real big trouble. Their affair had been going on for almost a year now. What started as some 'small time' flirting on the train and a bold step of fingers touching through the cut bogie, had blossomed into a love affair.

Aarti had told him little about herself, except that she had a brother . . . . Kiran . . . somewhere in Pirangut near Pune. They had gone out to a few movies and many outings in Marine drive, Siddhivinayak and Mahalakshmi temple's in Mumbai And so many weekends in Vile.

He had already taken her to meet his family in Ahmadabad. His parents had moved from Bombay to Ahmadabad after his father's retirement.

His home in Ahmadabad was small, and so they planned to leave in the evening. However, they stayed at a hotel in Ahmadabad after the evening train got canceled.

They went to the Navaratri garba and dandia . . . and later the light atmosphere . . . and one thing led to another, and they had gone all the way. Since then, they lived like a married couple but staying in two different homes.

There were so many memories.

He weighed it against the fact that her cousin was somewhere in the goon-political ladder. He'd have to talk with Aarti later and find out . . . .

Jay did not expect Aarti to be waiting in the station.

Was Andy serious about this girl?

There seemed to have been a lot of 'water under the bridge' . . . to use an Idiom . . . he had better find out. The girl was very beautiful. However, it seemed that her brother was mixed up in some gang somewhere near Pirangut, Pune and things could get ugly real soon.

How would Andy match up his middle-class parents with Aarti's goon family?

How could Andy get mixed up with such mess with relative ease?

Andy was handsome and Aarti beautiful, and they made a good pair. However, his flamboyant style of living . . . . that's where the trouble lies . . . . Why could he not be more introverted like the others?

Andy: "Aarti, this is Jay. My classmate and now my colleague for two years."

Aarti: "Andy speaks of you all the time. How are you?"?

Jay: "I'm fine. He never speaks about you with us. This has been like a secret . . . . What do I say now . . . This news has hit me like a thunderbolt . . . Lets have tea."

They walked into a nearby restaurant.

Jay: "Your cousin Bhiku called me today and threatened me a lot. He asked me to pass this message to Andy, and I didn't know that you'd be waiting in the station."

Aarti: "I should not have told Kamali. She has slipped in everything to Bhiku."

Andy: "OK. You'd not have imagined that she'd do this."

Jay: "Tell me the details of how long this has been going on and what are your plans."

Andy: "We met somewhere around a year ago. We fell in love and are quite dedicated to each other."

Jay: "Let's cut the chase short. Are you planning to get married?"

Aarti: "I assume so, but we have not talked about it yet."

Jay: "That's great. Now you guys have to make up your minds very quickly. When are you getting married?"

Aarti: "We never thought about this and never discussed."

Andy: "We do not want to rush to marriage. Our relationship is going on smoothly, but we have so many hurdles. Career at the beginning stage now, so not yet planned."

Jay: "You guys are not in the United States. This is India. Your cousin is likely to catch up with Andy shortly . . . and the only thing that can save his limbs are some concrete plans.

You have to be clear.

Either you have planned on getting married or this is off.

Aarti, you know your family better. You better put some sense into his head."

Aarti: "We did speak of marriage when we went to his home in Ahmadabad, but later his parents turned cold to our relationship and since then we have kept a lid on that topic."

Andy: "I want some more time. With the PTA 44 project in this state, holidays are impossible and any day, I may have to go to the site. You know how dangerous that place is. I don't want Aarti to face the uncertainty of the site. It's almost like a war zone."

Jay: "I think you are making too much of the one conflict and incident that happened there. We had the 26-11, but that doesn't make Mumbai a dangerous place to live. If the management were to ask you to go, just say 'No'."

Aarti: "We will have to give some date and tell them our intentions. That way, we will 'cross the tide' and buy us some time. We can always delay a little bit. But why can't we get married, and then you do all these things with your career? You know Andy, I would also like to support you in your career" Aarti felt a little more confident speaking out thus, as Jay was there . . .

Jay "Andy, this is very-very crucial now. You need to tell his cousin of some date in the near future. A day when you were going to come with your family to their home. And then let's get some date fixed. After all, you are serious about her. Are you not?"

Andy: "Yes of course! OK. We'll do that."

After some more small talk, they paid the tab and started walking out. However, Bhiku Patil and a couple of tough looking chaps were just outside the hotel and motioned them to enter a waiting SUV.

They got in. Bhiku started with a big lecture on morality and the likes to Aarti.

Bhiku: "Aarti, you know your family condition. How could you do all this?

You have been given all this freedom and liberty. To work in Bombay and live a life of your choice and you do something like this."

The conversation seemed out of the world to Andy at times. Born in a very cosmopolitan atmosphere in Mumbai, one could never expect something like this in Mumbai. Seemed like Aarti's family were very conservative.

Bhiku: "And you," now pausing in his lecture and posing a question to Andy, "you have come here to work or do all these things with girls here."

Andy: "Look bhai (brother) . . . . We are serious about each other and intend to get married soon. We were going to inform her family. She has already visited my family in Ahmadabad."

Aarti: "Bhau (brother), I have a right to decide about my life. You also have your girl friend and why do you feel that I should not have a right to decide on my life."

Andy: "In fact, fact my family has been asking a date on which to approach your family."

The talk of marriage cooled things down a little.

Bhiku: "What's this . . . like you mean that his family may be anybody. Andy, do you know about us? You should have properly approached and asked us. This alliance is not possible at all. This talk of Marriage is not possible!

Do you know about bhau (Kiran)? He is in the Sena . . .
Aawaj Kunacha! (who's voice rules!) . . ."

Andy: "Which Sena?"

That hurt a bit, the split in the Sena was a thorn in every
Marathi person's mind. The un-split Sena had been a pride
of the Maharashtrian's. Bhiku smiled a little, but he was
somewhat annoyed. "Yes, now we have two Sena's."

Soon, there were joined by another goon-looking
character, who probably spent most of his time in the
gyms and on fights.

"Kya Jay-bhai." It turned out that Jay and this guy had
played some cricket match, and he had asked Jay to join
their team for the Achanak cricket trophy. So they played
for the same team.

"You know him?" Bhiku asked.

"This is Jay. Remember I had told you about the guy who
had the idea of turning the 'Achanak cricket Saamna' into
an IPL like event."

"Ohh . . . yes!" Bhiku had liked the idea. "Someone
should take it to the next generation of the Sena leaders.
So this is the guy."

"Yes. It is a huge lost opportunity." Jay reiterated his
position.

The Acahanak cricket Saamna was conceived and
supported by the Sena. It was held in many grounds across
the state of Maharashtra, with minimal facilities. Jay had

played Acahanak matches right from the early days when there was no facility for such tournaments. You had very bad pitches where the ball would bounce unevenly. The pebbles in the unmaintained grounds would hurt the fielders.

Jay was of the opinion that the Sena should ask its channel partners to broadcast the local matches and rope in some advertisers and bring in some glamour and glitz and turn it into a show that every family could enjoy.

Remove some of the rough crowd and get more women involved in the organizing, which would help to rope in more family crowd to these matches. In the initial stages, plastic chairs need to be arranged for the family crowd to sit. Later there could be better arrangements. It could be a spectacle like a mini IPL and provide exposure to the lesser-known players living in every single village and town of India.

The small talk of cricket lightened the mood.

Bhiku: "I really do not know how Kiran will take to all this. He's in Sena. But I do not know how he will take it. He's a hot head. He will come down heavily on us. Do not tell him all this about Ahmadabad and things like that. I have no objection except that Aarti is our responsibility, as long as she is here. We will be blamed for a long time for this . . . They will say that we neglected her and did not give proper attention to details etc etc."

So they plotted some more on what and how to tell her brother so that the issue could be settled with relative ease.

Kiran came to know about the news from Bhiku. Bhiku could not keep this to himself. It would have been considered a betrayal of family values or some such thing.

Kiran immediately called and arranged for three guys to come with him to Mumbai. Kiran was a rising star in the Sena. He was worried, how would an alliance with a Gujarathi be looked upon by others and how that would affect his career?

Another Sainik had also evinced interest in Aarti . . . and Kiran and his mother were seriously considering the alliance.

Everything matched, and he may get a lot of political mileage out of the alliance in Pune.

He asked the fourth guy to bring the sack. The sack had a couple of hockey sticks and a couple of choppers and a sword.

He did not tell his mother about this so far. He did not know how she would take it.

How deep was his sister into this? He prayed to the stars that this was just a small flirt and that Bhiku had raised an unnecessary alert.

There were many 'smart alecks' in Mumbai. They thought nothing about having an affair. However, from where he came, if things happened without raising dust, then ok . . . but if things went awry, blood would flow quite easily . . .

He had to keep it quiet.

Get Aarti out of Mumbai.

Fix up the engagement and marriage quickly and then . . .

Should he call Aarti?

Better not do that.

Do it as quietly as possible.

If the boy came in between . . . Well there was the chopper . . . use it as a threat . . . Keep it cool . . .

He called Bhiku and informed him that he was starting from Pirangut. Bhiku informed him that they were in it (the affair) quite deep.

"Come here and then we'll talk about it."

"There's nothing to talk about. We'll warn the boy. If he still persists, rough him up a little bit. Show him some weapons and leave it at that."

"Let's be cool. You know, once the chopper is out; it has its own story to tell . . . you never know how one thing could lead to another. Come here and let's decide."

Bhiku weighed this for some time and gave an advance warning to Aarti.

"Bhau is angry. I do not know what will happen."

Andy was not hungry. The couple of Tea's and the events had kind of 'killed' his appetite. But as a rule he never punished his stomach for events that affected his head. Every evening he got his dinner from the "Khanaval" (a restaurant that provides dinner and lunch boxes to monthly customers). He looked at the fare and slowly dug into his food.

"Kya saab . . . Aaj Tension? (what sir, tensions today?)"

"Nothing. Just the regular."

"Just remember Guruji and leave your problems to him."?

Andy smiled. In fact, it was he who had asked the other to do the Part-1 course. Sudarshan kriya helped him keep his cool. That and Sahaj Samadhi Meditation technique had brought a sea of change to his life. It made him much more balanced and cool, . . . though he felt that there was still a long way to go.

He tried to remember all the problems and put them at Guruji's feet. PTA 44 schedule, OTS related issues, Feed mix automator, Relationship with Aarti. Well Guruji . . . solve all of them for me.

Sometimes when he did that, he felt that he was some kind of a beggar. He had at some point stopped asking god for these fringe benefits. He felt that god and guru had more to worry about than Andy.

Anyway, this 'leaving the problems at Guruji's feet', made him feel better. He started attacking his food. His mobile rang three beeps. He looked at the mobile. Three messages.

Aarti was not sure what would happen once she reached Pirangut. The moment Kiran arrived in Airoli, the atmosphere had turned somber.

What Kiran had done immediately was snatch her phone and get Andy's number from it. The phone was still in his pocket. This was a brother whom she did not know.

He paced the room like a tiger in its cage. His face was contorted with anger.

"How could you do this to us?"

"Bhau, what have I done. I'm in love with Andy, and we are going to get married."

"To you, we have suddenly become nothing. You do not think, what will happen once you are married to an outsider? We will be outcasts."

Suddenly, the phone rang. It was their mother. All Aarti could hear was him muttering "Ok . . . . Ok."

Then he announced, "We are immediately going to Pirangut."

There are many things that could happen. She knew that her family was seeking an alliance for her. This could intensify. They may be ready to compromise on the groom's looks and financial and social standing.

She had in the past felt that her mother and brother would understand her love and accept her decision. But she was not prepared for the abuses, and incriminatory remarks that were happening.

She had never anticipated the behavior that Kiran showed towards her.

Her only hope seemed to rest with her mother.

The discussions were not going anywhere.

The entire family in Airoli was on the defensive. It was like "What could we do?"

"She kept everything so close to her chest."

"We would never have let this happen, if we had known earlier."

"What's the use of educating girls, if they would be doing such mischief before their marriage?"

"Arey Saab, Khana kar lo baad mein dekho" (Sir, finish dinner and then look (at the messages)).

He finished his food. Maybe, there was a miracle and all problems were solved. He prayed and then looked at the messages.

Mani: The Automator needs resolution! There will be a big meeting tomorrow morning starting at 7:00. I have sent a request to Marshall and Paresh. Management will also be there.

Ramesh: I checked the CD. The latest program is already loaded. The date also matches. The training system is a mess. Meeting tomorrow at 7:00

Aarti: Bhau is here and I think that they will take me to Pirangut. Come to Pirangut directly and settle our marriage . . .

The gods are definitely not happy with me now! How am I going to be in three places at one time tomorrow morning? He set the alarm clock. Thoughts seemed to come in and go at a very high speed. The three complex issues facing him caught up his mind rapidly alternating, from one to next to the other. After some time, he could not think of any solution, but a repeat of the questions coming into his mind. Luckily, sometime in the night, he fell asleep.

##

They reached Pirangut late that night.

"Hey kay kelas?" Her mother started. ("What have you done?").

Before Aarti could say anything, her mother started crying. "After your father left us, I went through so much pain to bring you up. And I get rewarded like this. You are having affairs and spoiling the 'name of the family' (family's reputation) in Mumbai.

What will the people in Airoli think? We think so low of the morals of people in Mumbai, and now you go there and do this."

Her ranting continued for some more time. At the end of which Aarti felt more frustrated at her situation.

Once everyone was calm, she told them that she wanted to sleep and took her phone that was kept on the table now and started retiring to her room.

However, her mother started again. "Where are you going to sleep now? You have taken our sleep away and now you want to sleep."

Aarti talked about Andy and his parents.

"You know his parents." Then she told them about her visit to Ahmedabad to meet his parents. She saw a glimmer of hope. Maybe if she told everything about the affair, then she would probably kill their hopes of marrying her to any other boy. Slowly, she spilled the beans. She even exaggerated some of their trips, and though she could not talk about sex, she told them that she did not see anything wrong as they were going to get married and "everything was ok to do"

They kept telling her to stop thinking about Andy and tried to dash her hopes that Andy would marry her. She was alternately sobbing and at times emotionally strong, sometimes in control over the situation and at times felt desperately alone.

So the discussions went from one corner of the affair to another. Aarti stood her ground that Andy would marry her, and she would marry Andy.

While her mother and brother tried to tell her that they did not know Andy, but had enquired a little in the evening and it turned out that he had had a few girlfriends in the past and that it is possible that he may ditch Aarti.

Vultures are patient birds!

─◈─

They say life is fast in Mumbai. If life is fast in the city, then life is super fast in the suburbs.

Here, life starts very early. An hour's journey in the local trains is considered child's play. One and a half is a bit normal and more than that, and you need to rethink on life.

The 5 30 AM, local is not empty. You may get lucky and get a 4th seat. 4th seat is also a typical humanity that is shown in second class compartments in Mumbai locals. The 2nd class compartment has rows of three seats, but the three people would be expected to squeeze in, and a fourth person could get a very small place to sit in an awkward position.

The locals are generally "Jam-Packed"!

Andy looked at Jay, Surprised to find him coming in this early. Jay seemed unhappy.

'Kya Andy, tum logon ne aish kiya aur humko saza!" (you guys had the fun, and we get the punishment).

"Jay, nothing like all this happened." Something was seriously wrong. Jay hated to get up in the morning.

"Andy, I do not know what you guys did. After yesterday's 'event' with Aarti, I find it difficult to believe you. The situation looks bad. I know that you would have worked very hard, and so far everybody suspected Srinivas of having gotten a free ride, but now people are talking about you too."

"Jay, this is news to me. Do not believe anything that is being talked about. Trust me . . . . I spent almost 10-11 hours a day in office. And most of the Saturdays I was in. The USA guys found me very painful. I even had a few fights with them over working on weekends. You know how sensitive they are to that. Finally, we got the Pune guys working on weekends."

"Then why is nothing working, Andy? Everybody is talking now, and they are saying that Srinivas must have corrupted you. One rotten apple spoils the basket"

"Srinivas is Srinivas, but I am not a child. Srinivas had a good time there. But I covered up and did the entire routine diligently."

"Hey, is it true that he took a call from a strip tease."

"Ab kya bolun.(what should I say)"

"Tell me yaar (friend). After all, we are classmates."

"He used to disappear from work promptly at 4 30, putting in eight hours. Then, he would go to some strip tease joint. Early-bird discounts and stuff like that. One of the girls also visited him at the hotel. One evening, the conference call was late, and he forgot about it. He was in the striptease, and we called his cell. He remembered about the call when his phone rang.

Then he went into the toilet . . . . because in other areas, the music is so loud . . . and took the call."

"Baap re! Salaam to him! You need some nerve." Both laughed for some time . . .

"Yes! Then he would find opportunities to run to Houston. He knew this joint in Houston which he used to call 'Khazana'. A treasure chest, or Jannat or heaven. And to top that, when he was in office, and I was working, he'd be searching the net for fetish items, sex toys and what not. He even visited a store in Atlanta and got a lot of pillows and other stuff, Sex furniture, some fiber material that would tickle your back and what not. One pillow for rocking sex! Man that dude is a sex maniac."

"Oh my god! He had gone on an official visit to Atlanta."

"I know. But this is strictly between you and me."

"You have my word. But people are saying that his head will roll today. Haresh and Ramesh will demand this. You will have to take sides. Man, this is big trouble. Somehow, though he is a rascal in many-ways, the audacity of what he does, and the way he treats people makes Srinivas dear."

"I hope that he tides over these issues."

"These guys are all Vultures. Waiting on a prey and they are very patient. And it looks like Srinivas is going to be devoured . . . . These Vultures are certainly patient birds.

They will probably have his dead meat today. Anyway tell me some more details."

"One day these guys dragged me to a joint in Houston. One of the girls, I guess is a college student, and it seems she knows Srinivas. Maybe because of his frequent visits.

He goes 'Hi Maria.'

'Hi my darling engineer.' Heavy Mexican accented English.

They sit together holding hands, and soon they go to upstairs. That is a special zone for regulars like him. Where she seems to have given him head.

Anyway later, he comes down, and on napkins; he explains his cross version of Kamasutra (ancient Indian treatise on sex) and Trignometry theory of sex. He draws so many lines and angles and types of girls and men as described in Kamasutra. He explains to her how all the ancient theories and positions combined with modern science, and mathematics ties up to give heightened pleasures and sensations. He has the girl pretty much hooked. Next weekend, she drives to Austin, and for two days they are practicing all that they had discussed."

Ha Ha. Both were again laughing at this.

"And one day after his visit to Atlanta, he has brought this huge somewhat semicircular pillow called 'Scoop'. And he is passionately discussing over the phone with someone at the pillow manufacturing company. I could hear him explain, how having two scoops with straps could be better design. He even had a CAD draftsman draw some designs and sent it to Atlanta.

At times, I would be embarrassed. During an official dinner, he goes off on the topic of sex dolls. He says that all automation guys are sleeping, and this grand opportunity is passing us by.

Add automation to the new dolls. He is 'gung-ho' about dolls with some silica tissue with skeletons. SFC's and Sequencers used in automation are wasted on meaningless processes, he goes.

He describes, how complex SFC's and Sequencers can be used to program these sex dolls with a lot of robotics and automation added to it.

He describes the sequences and how the experience will be beyond those possible with other humans. Then on his Smartphone, he pulls out a catalogue of a company that makes dolls. Each like a super model or actress.

He is so excited, he describes how actual voice and words could be added and along with the automation and sequences described, he declares that humans would have their first Droid's or sex droids. Sex Droids are the future of human companionship! So he declares.

Finally, he summarizes, that in future, humans or a person would have several such droids modeled after their favorite stars and models and with custom selectable features.

I mean, his tehno-droid yarn dominates the dinner. And that too with all managers and directors of the vendor present. I tried to divert the topic, but the guys at the table regard him as some nerdy technical genius. Somehow due to his technical skills, he gets away with it."

"Not today. The vultures have been patiently waiting for a long time. Now they have him in a corner. They will flock on him and devour him. He's dead meat.'

"I am not going to say anything against him. Though this is one part of his personality, and that he never works overtime, etc. He was always in office during office hours, and he was key to testing and debugging the training system. Without him, we would be having a lot of issues here"

"I guess that's why people are involving your name. Kind of try to get you to spill the beans on Srimivas."

"I am not going to squeal. But why are you up so early?"

"I am supposed to be supporting you. This means that they see no alternative to you and plan to groom me to be that alternative. But I have made it clear that I do not want to be involved or be part of a takeover."

"Hmnnn."

"Is mein kush nahin hain." (There is nothing in this now). Jay knew that the only thing left in this project was hard work. All the tours, the trainings and perks were finished. Actually, Jay felt that Ramesh would have been better off with Srinivas on the lead till the end. By trying to nail Srinivas, they would succeed in some goal, but end up doing all the hard work in this project.

But he kept his opinions to himself. If he got dragged into this, then he could end up doing all the hard work. Put in the long hours and be responsible for every deliverable.

He did not like the scene.

Showcause . . .

"Andy, I have to serve you a show cause notice." Mani said.

"Show Cause! But why?" Andy was shocked beyond belief. He had come to work with a serious belief that he had to perform some miracle to save Srinivas.

And to find that he was in the line of fire and not Srinivas, was a shocker.

Every company has an ethics policy. A watchdog of the company, its officers and employees. In old days, there was a vigilance department and their chief objective was to keep graft under check. Vigilance officers were like detectives in the organization. Things were done by the good old methods.

As time passed, companies adopted the American model. There was an ethics department, a third party agency that took in ethics complaints and resolved them. Company officials had been sacked in the past for minor infringements. People had always been afraid of the ethics policy.

And as a rule, people always expressed their concern to their immediate superior. And if there was merit in their complaint, the supervisor might have called in the concerned employee and counsel him. No employee had gone and complained in the ethics portal so far.

What Subba had done was unthinkable. Overnight he had shaken the entire hierarchy. His complaint was against the whole team.

Mani was annoyed at Srinivas. That old oaf!

Why did he have to be a hero?

Why not keep things under the lid?

Why tell people of his escapades?

He had already tried to reprimand Srinivas on several occasions in the past. But Srinivas was Srinivas. Mani realized that Srinivas would probably never change.

Srinivas was a prized asset of the team. He was very intelligent, and the complete setup and growth had been through his ideas. Mani owed him many times. Every time, they were in a corner, one of Srinivas's ideas or suggestions pulled them out.

He could also draft some good letters explaining situations, be it an extension of a shutdown or a new concept or budget extensions. He could think of things, that no one could. He could visualize and find solutions, when everyone turned blank. He had done so many things for the company.

Mani carefully read the letter submitted in the ethics portal. The letter talked specifically about the training system, and that it was not working. This had been the responsibility given to Andy. He felt that Andy could get away with this complaint.

There would be an inquiry for sure. Subba had put them in a deep hole.

He had had great expectations from Subba. However, he had played into the hands of Ramesh.

That slimy bastard!

However, Mani appreciated Ramesh's skills. He had killed two birds with one stone!

Ramesh was not an intellectual, but where he lacked in thinking about something new, he adequately made up with diligently following procedures and protocols. He was a hard-working individual and was tenacious. He would spend hours on any aspect unknown. He would be the first to study a new project and know everything about it, while Srinivas could skim through the project details and throw a hundred ideas, issues and items that no one else could see so soon, Ramesh would know every published detail of the project.

Ramesh's hard-working methods were an inspiration to others in the organization. Organizations depended on loyal, hardworking people like him. He inspired people to stay long hours in the office, while Srinivas could hardly manage the daily boredom of the eight hours.

They complemented each other.

Mani was lucky to have such varied personalities working for him.

Subba was a disappointment. He had the skills and tenacity, but he should not have bypassed the hierarchy. Mani was sure that Subba had been misled by others into this misadventure.

This thing was not done! Subba would have to learn his lessons the hard way.

Mani felt that he had to save Srinivas. He should take Srinivas to task at some other time. Mani had to groom him so that he would not become an unnecessary liability to him and the organization.

"Subba has crossed the limit this time. He has gone ahead and put up a complaint against the team in the ethics portal. He is saying a lot of blah . . . blah . . . , but his main concern is that the training software is not working. This was your responsibility, Andy . . . . So I have no choice."

Andy was not sure that Subba had complained against him, but if what Mani said was right, then Subba had actually put him in a spot.

Andy could not believe that Subba could have done this to him.

But then why would Mani be saying so? Subba has gone too far. Complain against him in the ethics portal.

Rage anger and frustration rose in Andy. After all those hours of hard work, he was getting a 'show cause" notice. He could not believe it.

"Sir, the software was working and every change was made. This is bullshit!!!" He was enraged. His voice choked with emotion and almost in tears.

"Relax" Mani got up and kept a hand on Andy's shoulder. He handed him a glass of water to drink. "Well, right now the complaint says that the training software is not working. And that you have somehow screwed all this up. I do not believe what he has written, but he has leveled some serious allegations against you. The first thing would be to draft a reply to the Show Cause. Srinivas, help Andy out on this. We do not want it to be defensive.

Now, is the Training software working or not? If it is working, then you have nothing to really worry about." Mani was careful now.

"It is working fully (which is the Indian way of saying that everything in the software was performing as per the specifications). I vouch for that. I know what these guys (Andy and team) have done. I have tested each and every aspect and reported all the bugs and got them resolved." Srinivas intervened.

"Well then that is good. But we do not want to play on this right now. Let us get the people to vent their anger.

If Srinivas says, that the software was working, then I believe that it was working.

Srinivas, the first thing is to answer to the Showcause notice.

I am deeply disappointed at Subba. I always thought he was very balanced."

"Sir, it is not Subba. The words themselves have a tinge of 'Ramesh' written over it. Ramesh has been gunning (me) because he did not get to go." Srinivas continued.

"Hmnn . . . Well any ways, the first thing is to get the reply drafted. Who is Subba reporting to?"

"Sir, he is reporting to Ramesh right now. Though officially he is under Ramesh, the administrative rights are still with me"

"Okay. Andy can you make a first draft reply on this ShowCause Notice and come back quickly. Do not talk with anyone until you are done."

"Yes Sir." Andy left.

"So you have all the administrative rights.

"First thing, Srinivas I want you to sober down a little bit. Do you want to grow in this organization or do you want to be reporting to Ramesh or Subba very soon?"

"Sir, I will be happy to work under you. Under anyone else, it will be impossible. You know, I cannot play company politics. I am a straight shooter."

"Srinivas, I have guided you and saved you from these vultures many a times. You have the potential to grow beyond me, if only you can speak less with the normal people. Keep things to yourself."

"I will try."

"Good. What's your take on Subba?"

"Sir, he is a hard worker. A loose cannon at times, but Ramesh has used him."

"Nevertheless, we cannot let this happen. I want people to firmly know that we are the administration here. I don't want people doing things as per their wishes, coming and leaving at their wish.

I want you to do the following.

Subba should not get any Leave's that are discretionary. CL etc . . . On every sick leave insist on a doctor's certificate. On EL we will follow company rules. If he is applying 15 days in advance, then we can think of. Even if he applies two months in advance, your approval will come only 15 days in advance.

No travel trips even to Ghansoli. If he goes out for an hour, then he should be reprimanded.

I want him to know that we are the administrators here, and we have a role to play.

He cannot bypass us and go to some management portal.

What does he think?

I am nobody here.

I am sitting here to swat flies!

He gets no perks, and all our discretionary powers are used to make him uncomfortable.

Do you get me?"

"Yes Sir, but won't he object?"

"Let him."

"Srinivas, I have diverted the complaint and used a few sentences against the training software to mean Andy. But this was written against you. You need to be more careful. Your mistakes can land others in deep trouble."

"Thanks sir. I will do everything to protect Andy"

Andy could not believe the turn of events. And neither could anybody from Jay to Ramesh to Subba.

Of course, Subba had mentioned the training system, and Andy was responsible for it.

Everyone was feeling miserable.

Andy looked at the Showcause notice.

Date 14 Oct

To,
Andy,

Employee No. 11375,
Sub: Show Cause Notice

It had been brought to the attention of the Management that "The training software" for PTA44 project—OTS system is not working.

It is also alleged that you have willfully misled personnel at Ghansoli, showing wrong progress information and queries that misled them to believe that there were genuine issues with the software.

Kindly explain why further disciplinary actions like suspension from service or termination should not be initiated against you.

Please respond within 48 hours giving your explanation to avoid initiation of further disciplinarian actions against you.

Mani K
AVP PTA operations.

What should he write? He could only think of 'gaalis' or bad words. He could not write that. He should think of a counter attack.

He started scribbling a reply.

> *This complaint is chiefly due to the fact that*
> *Subba was not sent to America.*

Was 'chiefly' a correct word? Or should he use 'Mainly' or alter the sentence.

Indians had a love for 'ly'. Parallel became 'parallelly' and he had come to know very late in life that 'Parallelly 'was wrong and it should be 'in parallel to'.

But he also thought that maybe someday with its prolific use, Parallelly would find its way to some dictionary.

He struck out that line and started again.

> ~~*This complaint is chiefly due to the fact that*~~
> ~~*Subba was not sent to America.*~~

> *Dear Sir,*
> *The complaint was raised by Subba, mainly*
> *because he did not get to go to America.*

Should he leave it at that? This was not time to be a sissy. He recollected that someone had said 'Attack is the best form of defense.'

Further, Subba has been going home early from the inspection at Thane and is the reason, why he thinks, everyone is like him.

Let the ass hole burn. He remembered the movie Fahrenheit 911 . . . What was the song that was played in their helmets . . . .

Die Mother f@@$%r die . . . .

His spirits renewed.

If Subba could try to screw him, let that guy know that everybody has a dick, and Subba could get counter screwed!

Subba along with a senior had written this complaint after willfully destroying the software and loading the old software.

There is one more backup at the central locker.

Once this is loaded then the software will work.

Please do not take cognizance of the complaint and retract this show cause notice.

Thanks and best regards!
Andy

'That's it Subba' Andy's mind spoke . . .' You will burn with the consequence of your complaint.'

Die Mother f@@$%& die . . . .

Que Sera Sera

A ndy felt some remorse later. Maybe he should not have attacked Subba so vehemently. He should retract and rewrite. However, he needed to do something about Aarti.

He was literally at a "Trishanku" state . . . Ha Ha . . . Three problems . . . Trishanku . . . .

He could not think very straight.

How could Subba have done this to him? Andy asked himself again. Jay had been wrong about Subba. Subba, was not after Srinivas, but after Andy!

He had to go to Pirangut and be with Aarti.

Suddenly, he felt some vibration in his pocket. His mobile! OMG (Oh My God) . . . he had forgotten all about it.

He took it out, and he saw that there were 12 missed calls from Aarti!!

Before he could take the phone out of silent mode, it rang again.

"Why are you not picking up the phone?" Aarti demanded.

"Aarti, I was in a meeting."

"We are in deep trouble and all you can think of is work? I told you to come directly to Pirangut"

"Aarti, I'm in very deep trouble at work."

"Andy my brother has gone to Pune to talk with the other groom

They want to arrange my marriage quickly."

She started sobbing.

"Aarti, I will apply for leave tomorrow . . . ."

"Why tomorrow? . . . Why not next month? You apply for leave next year and come directly to my child's birth event! Here I am not able to live for one second. Every second is dragging like ages, and you want to come next year" she was sobbing more ferociously. "My brother was saying that you will not come. I will never understand a man's world. You would not be interested in me anymore . . ."

All the brainwashing done by mother and brother and the seeds of doubt that they had sown last night was taking its effect. Aarti suddenly started feeling very insecure.

"Arey . . ."

"All men are alike. My brother and mother have been bothering me the whole night, and you are saying that you will come after your office people are happy."

"Aaga . . . ."

"Do you love me?"

"Is that a question to ask? hunh . . ?"

"If you start saying that you will come so late, I have to ask . . . na . . . No . . . Answer me right now!" ('na' is typically used in Mumbai English, which seeks confirmation from the other person)

"Yes."

"Then nothing doing! Just drive straight to my home and take me away from here. If that guy says 'yes', then I will have no option but to die. I cannot think of living with anyone but you."

"But . . . ."

"No Andy, no 'buts'! Come here immediately."

She hung up.

He changed the mode silence mode to general mode and called Aarti, but she cut off the phone.

He saw Jay coming into the room.

"I have to go."

"Where?"

"Pirangut."

"What! Are you out of your mind?"

"Maybe."

"Look I talked with Subba. He is very sorry. They wanted to attack Srinivas. But Mani has misunderstood the entire thing and got you involved.

Andy, you should focus on the reply to the show cause notice. Are you listening to what I have to say? Andy, you could be losing your job here!"

"Jay, why are we working? Tell me why? Why did we struggle and become engineers?

To keep ourselves and family happy. But if that cannot happen, then what is the point? I worked the entire duration in USA, like an ass.

Slogged 12 hours or more a day and see what I got in return."

"Andy don't be stupid. You do not get jobs like these every day. Just calm down. For all you know there could be some goons with choppers and knives waiting for you in Pirangut."

Andy had not considered this. Yes, there was a threat to his life.

He tried Aarti's number again.

"Andy, please do not call again and again. My mother is continuously lingering around me. At times, I have to go to the toilet and speak into the phone. Just come here and take me away from here."

"OK."

Andy felt that, that was that. He could not take any more of this situation. It was time to go to the Battlefront and wage war!

"Jay, que-sera-sera! Whatever will be, will be. I must go now."

He forgot to send the letter by email.

Jay walked into Subba's cabin Ramesh and Subba were discussing the next move.

Jay "Hi guys."

Ramesh "You told Andy that we were after Srinivas, and this whole thing has backfired."

Jay "I think until you two make a move to rectify this, there is no way Andy is going to be happy."

Ramesh knew that if his people felt that he had been responsible for anything that impacted Andy, they would not be happy. These two would become a pariah, and others would be wary and antagonized.

He had to dissociate himself from this event.

"I have a meeting with Mani and have to update him on the status of the feed mix Automator. We will all go and discuss with Mani. Maybe he will see the light and issue show cause to Srinivas."

That renewed some hope in Jay. Andy needed to be out of this trap.

They moved somberly to Mani's cabin.

Mani somewhat curtly acknowledged their presence. He was visibly annoyed at them.

"Sir, we wanted to take a few minutes to discuss the complaint before we start the discussion on the feedmix." Ramesh started in a low voice.

"What is there to discuss? I have issued show cause notice to Andy, and he has to reply to it." Mani was visibly irritated. Jay felt that this had not been that good of an idea, but he could do nothing now.

"Sir . . ."

"Subba, I thought that you and Andy were good friends. If you saw something going wrong, you should have advised Andy and then reported to me, and we would have acted early to bridge the gap."

"Sir, The complaint was against Srinivas and not Andy." Subba felt that this was the opening he wanted and seized the opportunity to clear Andy.

Ramesh was visibly unhappy. This statement would put him in bad light, as if he were 'ganging up' against Srinivas. However, he kept quiet.

"That is preposterous. You have complained that the team that went there did not do their job. That they were often sighted in dance bars and other such places and neglected the entire training software changes. Am I wrong?"

"No sir." Subba was quiet.

"Andy was responsible for the entire training software thing. If it is not working, then Andy is answerable. It is a crystal clear matter."

"But sir, Srinivas was the senior-most person on the team, and he should have taken the initiative." Ramesh intervened.

"Come-on Ramesh. The agenda items in Srinivas's itinerary were finalized by yourself and me. In fact, you added so many items, and I felt that he would not be able to complete any. And last week, you yourself commended him on a job well done."

"Sir, I wanted to complain against Srinivas and not Andy. I will withdraw the complaint." Subba offered.

"What do you guys think this is? Some circus being run by the MD! You have complained on the ethics portal. There is an independent agency that overlooks the complaints there.

Last month, MD had been talking of closing this contract and reducing the ethics budget as there has so far been no complaint.

Now you make use of the portal for your personal grudges!

Now, those guys will spend a lot of time and money investigating this complaint of yours.

This is a big dilemma to me and management.

Do you know what will happen now?

All travel will be restricted. Those who do travel will have to send in umpteen reports. Every action will be super analyzed.

Even MD would be personally looking into this complaint.

Why did you at least not talk to me before doing all this mischief?"

"Sir, I thought that with the training software not working, there was some merit in this. We even had a meeting with Andy yesterday."

"So, what was the outcome?"

"Sir, he says that the training software is working."

"Even Srinivas says so. That being the case, then this complaint is baseless."

"But the training software is not working, and I have evidence that Srinivas was at . . . ." Subba defended the complaint.

"Look guy's, where Srinivas went or did not go does not help this complaint. It has no bearing on this matter, so to speak . . . This is about the Training software not working!

Ramesh, why did you guys not come to me first? At the onset, this complaint looks personally motivated. You have used the system to put down someone. I cannot go to the management with this.

All our promotions and everything that this department has achieved will be impacted.

The wolves at the corporate office will devour us.

Ramesh, even the gods forbade the use of the 'Brahmastra'. (Brahmastra was like a divine weapon that would destroy everything like a hydrogen bomb or nuclear weapon) Do you know why? Nobody can escape unscathed, once the Brahmastra is used. Everyone will be affected.

This Brahmastra will impact all of us.

Leave rules will get strict. Everyone will want to know every detail of who is doing what, during all company trips.

Frankly, if the complaints are found true, action will be against Andy. Otherwise, all of us will suffer!"

Everybody was silent for some time. The uncertainty about the outcome and the possible fallouts overwhelmed their thoughts for some time.

"Anyway Jay, where is Andy? He was supposed to give a reply to the show cause notice."

"Sir," Jay intervened, "he had a family emergency and had to urgently go to Pune."

"What! What could be more important than answering the show cause notice? I'll never understand this young generation. I have had enough of this complaint for the day!

Any ways Ramesh, we need to discuss the feed mix automator issue."

Paradise for "Nature-Lovers" . . .

The road to Pirangut from Mangaon is very beautiful when it rains and when it is winter, the serenity of the Mulshi lake draws people from Pune to come and picnic on its banks.

The curved road from Mangaon to Vile (pronounced Vilay) is very scenic, you could be passing through what was once a forest. Every now and then you'd see signboards like 'vedi wakadi valane' which Aarti had informed him meant, 'Crazy twists and turns' and the road was somewhat narrow in most places and very narrow at some places.

Due to the Vile Bhagad MIDC coming up near Vile, the roads were being widened.

The best place to have food there is at the Gold Valley sector A's Orchard restaurant. The Ambience is almost five star quality. Air-conditioned restaurant, western and very clean restrooms, a mini play ground and swimming pool and gym adorn the foothills of the Tamhini ghat. The bungalow's built in Konkan style, using the "Jambha Dagad" or large red stone bricks that were a specialty of the Konkan-Ratnagiri region, remind one of an era of serene village life.

Andy had wondered, "why the air-conditioning in this area?" and Aarti had informed that the stone surfaces of the mountains or the Sahayadri's here were rich in some ferrite material and reflected the sun's heat.

"What do you mean by 'reflects'? You mean radiates"

"'Reflects re baba . . . . You have to stay here to experience it.' ('re baba' is a typical Marathi phrase, typically used to stress or reiterate something.)

And so they had rented a bungalow for two days, and Andy noticed that when the sun came out, the rocks reflected or radiated the sun's heat. It was almost like being in an open-air Sauna. Some of this could have been due to the summer season.

Luckily, the sun moved to the other side of the bungalow, and Andy and Aarti, put a couple of chairs in the shade of the bungalow and enjoyed getting 'heated up' by the giant rocks. They would go in and make love and come back and sit in the shade again.

Andy had packed the folding chairs that he had purchased at Walgreens during his last trip, and they had taken out the cooler. By evening, they consumed almost three liters of their favorite soda.

That had been fun.

They had since then, rented homes for weekends on several occasions.

The valley was beautiful and during rains, these very mountains seemed to halt the clouds on their onward journey.

Aarti had said that these mountains were like sentries, posted to halt the clouds.

"Those clouds that pay the 'hafta' (weekly protection money) can pass, else they have to pour here. And they make beautiful waterfalls along the way."

Andy could sight almost 15-20 waterfalls, falling from the top of the mountains. A sight that seemed right out of some Hollywood movie like 'Avatar'. Then they had driven ahead and seen the waterfalls on the Ghat roads. These many waterfalls where you could find picnickers reminded one of places like Malshej ghat or Khandala ghat. You could see people sitting on the rocks as rain water flowed down the mountain, so very near the state highway.

The road had a small stone parapet called "Katta" in local language built by the British to save the vehicles from falling off the cliffs.

They had spent one evening on this katta, Aarti with her legs hanging out facing the ravine, while Andy sat with his feet firmly on the ground facing the road and twisted his body to see the sun setting behind the hills beyond.

They had taken pictures outside the bungalow. Giving different poses, some like a 'yogi' sitting in meditation or in different mudra's (different postures of the hands) . . . Pictures of the sun setting at a distance, but looking as if it was doing so between the bungalows.

Andy at times, felt that this was childish, but Aarti insisted and tried different techniques. One where he held his palms facing upwards while she had bent at a strange angle and clicked, and it seemed as if Andy was holding up the setting sun. That had been their favorite picture and Andy had put this one up, as his profile picture.

After his lunch, Andy wanted to pay the bill and rush towards Pirangut. But he was yet to be served the ice-cream. Andy remembered, that on one occasion, they had expressed displeasure when the restaurant staff informed them that there was no ice cream. 'Expressed displeasure' being a mild way of putting it, well . . . Andy never knew that Aarti could fight this much.

They had been served two ice creams on the next meal.

He could see the now dry waterfalls and the katta and everything reminded him of the time spent with Aarti.

After you reach the top of the mountain, there is a temple which is in a bit secluded spot, and the foliage is quite thick, giving it a forest like appearance.

Andy had felt uncomfortable, being in a remote place like that temple. But after their prayers, Aarti had insisted that they walk into the forest, and he had objected.

"Just a few more steps."

"It's too secluded. If any wild animals come . . ."

"Wild animals! Ha Ha . . . We are the only 'wild ones' here."

"OK. Let's go back to the bungalow." Andy was seized by some kind of fear. He suddenly recollected scenes from many Hindi movies and imagined so many things that could go wrong in such remote secluded places . . .

"No. You come here and walk with me and get rewarded."

"Zidd mat kat!" (Don't act adamant).

"Come with me . . . OK! You wait here, and I will go alone."

Andy followed her. The forest and the chirping of insects increasing his nervousness . . . .

Aarti slowed down, and he thought that they would return. So he stopped as Aarti retraced her steps, a small mischievous smile on her face. Aarti came near him and kissed him and hugged him with 'animal' ferocity that indicated heightened passion and made Andy forget all those fears.

"We are now 'Nature Lovers'" she had kidded adding extra stress on the 'lovers' part of the sentence. Aarti's English was not perfect. However, she would think of some such crazy connotations and over a period of time, they had created their own library of code words.

"Or we are lovers in nature"

"That doesn't rhyme."

"The blue Lagoon!"

"Jab pyar kiya to darna kya."(why be afraid when you are in love. Name of a movie and a very popular Hindi song)

Making meaningless jokes they had walked back to their car.

"Oh Devi! (Godess) Please help us through this phase. We will come often and pray to you, and I will break 11 coconuts if things work out well." Muttering this Andy made a promise and thus bribed god to help them through.

The road becomes narrow and winds through a forest landscape. So dense is the foliage here, that even in peak summer, you are better off with the headlights on.

Then you come into a place where four mountains end in a ravine. It almost looks as if four elephants are huddled together in a conference. In all his travels, Andy had never seen such a mountain formation. He had in the past, taken many pictures of this spot and posted on Facebook.

Many state transport buses, and tourists halt here and look at the natural beauty, take some snaps and move on their journey.

Then there are mountains shaped like the ones in Texas and lakes and stuff like that.

"In any other country, this place would be famous and flocking with Tourists. But here . . . Nothing."

"It's good na . . . . (na is already explained) We get to enjoy it . . . pristine beauty."

Andy chuckled. "But think of all the lost opportunity."

"If everything gets developed, then what would happen to nature LOVERS like us." And she started giggling and it spread to him, and soon they were in an unstoppable mirth, like small schoolchildren they had giggled and laughed for a long time. A 'sight' to the people who had got outside the bus at that time and were staring at them . . . Crazed Mumbaikars . . .

Everything reminded Andy of the time spent here in the past.

He prayed that there were no chopper wielding goons waiting to receive him in Pirangut.

The thought sent a cold sweat down his spine. He had to convince Aarti's mother about their intentions and things would work out. Once she was in the bag, then he could tackle her brother. However, if she remained unconvinced, all his worst fears would turn out true.

In some ways, it was stupid of him to run away to Pirangut without answering the Showcause notice.

He should have talked with Srinivas and rewritten the Showcause. He prayed that things should settle down at his work place.

And what of the Feed Automator? He had stopped thinking of that entirely . . . .

I'm in a mess.

Collateral Damage

After his meeting with Ramesh, Mani called Srinivas and asked him to drop by.

"What is your take on the Training software."

"It is working. I'm one hundred percent certain."

"Then why is it not working now?"

"Ramesh must have screwed up the software files deliberately." Srinivas did not want to lose this opportunity.

"Srinivas, I only have your word for it. And I also am hearing bad news on the automator"

"What's wrong with it?"

"Looks like there is very less space, and we cannot fit it into the available space."

"Let me have a look at the drawings."

"I already did. The guys who went to the site seem to have 'goofed' it up. They missed some beams and structure in the drawings."

"We paid for that trip."

"Yes I know. I signed the approval. And Andy had so strongly recommended it."

"What can Andy do if the vendor screws it up?"

"I know that you feel strongly about this chap. But is he a good judge of people and what to do? Or has he been led to this outcome by the vendor."

"Sir, the boy is a 'gem'. He can think of solutions very fast and can put in the effort needed to make a project a success."

"I know Srinivas. However, if there are multiple screw-ups like this, then it could actually be better if the training software did not work. Kind of seals the deal for management"

Srinivas knew that sometimes it necessitated having a scapegoat. He envied Mani, because he could easily digest such decisions.

Was Andy's time up?

Collateral damage . . . that's what some called it.

If the Ethics complaint was proven wrong, then management would have to look at other aspects. One thing would lead to another. The other units and departments would smell blood and like sharks in the movie 'Jaws', they would be on their prey.

This was just the beginning of the clamor.

"He's a very hardworking boy, and this is not his fault." Srinivas tried to stand up for Andy.

"I Know Srinivas, but with Subba using this Brahmastra, we have no choice.

The complaints are quite serious. I hope that the training software is not too screwed up."

"The training software is working, and I have seen it working. So I believe it."

"But with the turn of events, it would be better that it had some small glitches that made it appear as not working. Else, we will be under different kinds of scrutiny and trouble."

"I think that you fret and think too complex. Once the training software is working, this complaint can be wiped out."

"I wish I had lived in a black-and-white world and could believe in it as you do."

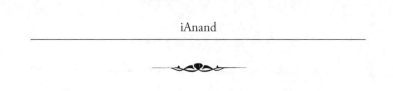

Srinivas looked at the napkins stored in his desk. Initially, the girl had not believed what he had told her. Thinking of it, as some ruse, to get her to go to bed with him for free.

But Srinivas was just displaying his knowledge of the adult sciences that he has assimilated. He had studied Kamasutra like a scientist studies nuclear physics. He had also studied some human anatomy and subscribed to a sex website and seen some of their training videos.

In one of the video's he had acquired the knowledge of the G spot. And he had added three sciences, Vatsayana's Kamasutra, Human anatomy and vector mathematics to make a 'killer' combination of techniques.

He had procured several sex pillows and furniture. The best of the category seemed to be from Atlanta.

He had seen videos, procured many fetish tools and pillows and studied positions as various angles. He had even invented a hypothetical force of one stroke and put up a name like "One thrust power".

His theory was that an accurate measurement of the G-spot from the mouth of the female sex-organ and calculation of your own angle and adjustments with the wedge pillow could offer calculated sensations to the woman. The thrust power had to be varied, and that would cause different sensations. The natural harmonics in nature and various angles with different thrust methods could hit the G spot in certain harmonically 'differentiated' force, and that could cause peak sensations.

He also had a technique where could hold his breath and along with a "Kapal Bhati" like (Kapal Bhati is a pranayama technique) action, and this caused a 'hammer' movement of his erect organ. He actually constricted his abdominal muscles and did the routine. That could be a hammer like horizontal motion in that confined space.

"Eureka!!", what he could do was tap on the G spot.

He had felt extremely restless on making this most important discovery while in Austin.

He had to publish this!

No . . . wait he had to try and prove his theory!

What an important invention or discovery this is!

How could he tell the world? But first he had to successfully prove his theory.

And this girl would not believe him. Why did he need to explain to her? Why not just demonstrate to her the forces and harmonics and his lateral hammering sensations, combined with the wedge pillow. Should be a perfect combination? But he felt that she should have the knowledge that he was going to hit the G spot, and her focus on that would be key to her understanding and 'differentiating' the orgasm.

Anyway, she found him interesting in a nerd kind of way and on his invite, she had come to Austin

Doing it to a professional . . . a professional he equated with the courtesans of ancient India. He imagined someone as knowledgeable as 'Vasantsena' of ancient India. Someone, who had to be conversant with the 'Kamasutra' and various Asanas (tantric and yogic postures) and the complete 'Kama-Shastra' or practice of love.

Anyway, much to his chagrin, as it turned out, the girl was a novice. The moment he had touched the G spot, she had an orgasm . . . and she was turned on so badly, that he need not have exercised even 10% of his skills.

When his moment came, to demonstrate his thrust power harmonic theory and hammer-tapping on the G spot, she was already solid gone. She did not understand the difference between the different waves of pleasure. She just knew that she had had a most wonderful experience.

He had married Malathy and Malathy had been sore at all this sexual experimentation. She called him a sex maniac. Hell! She did not know what she was getting daily.

He looked at the trigonometric drawings again. Such an advanced theory and practice! Where would he find his 'Vasantsena'. Would his practices be understood and appreciated in this world!

The world needed, the next 'Vatsayana'. He could be one, but this society, drawn from Victorian values would not understand. He could only get a 'sex maniac' label.

The world needed to stop focusing on religion and fundamentalism and start focusing on what could benefit every bedroom in every corner of the world. A knowledge that would have universal significance.

Mani entered his Cabin and that disturbed Srinivas's chain of thoughts . . .

"Hey, did you help Andy draft the letter?"

"No, I have not seen him."

"What are you doing then?"

"Just going through some drawings."

"Have you seen what Andy has written."

Mani showed him the copy of the reply that Andy had written.

"I thought he was out."

When Mani came to know that Andy was out, he had immediately summoned Jay and had asked him to see if Andy had written a reply and to send it to him. Jay started the department computer and luckily Andy had stored in a common folder. He quickly sent it to Mani.

Srinivas read and said 'Good, so that's what these 'holier than thou' bastards have been up-to.'

He would take those guys to task, next time. He should get Andy to spill some more secrets.

"What 'good'! Do you guys live in a literally Bollywood world? This is not some gang-war happening in the streets of Mumbai, where they give one blow and you the next."

Srinivas was showing his teeth. Somewhat lost in thoughts of how he would get Ramesh 'red-faced' over tea in the canteen, the next day. He remembered the ACDC song 'got you by the balls . . . .'

"Stop that idiotic grin. Your gang-war with Ramesh can wait. This is not the time to be fighting and shouting like women in a common pipeline, fighting over water."

In many slums in India, there is a common water pipe and one often sees women quarreling and fighting over who gets to fill water first and stuff like that in Indian movies.

Srinivas closed his mouth to stop showing his teeth, but could not stop his mind. His mirth was evident on his face.

Mani shook his head.

"Ask Andy to redraft. Ask him to just say that the accusations are wrong and submit your timesheets and that the loaded software was incorrect. And for god's sake ask him to get the training system working."

"What's wrong with what he has written?" Srinivas did not want Ramesh to go unscathed.

"Srinivas, this is not a gang-war. This is work. If you want to take over the reins, you should learn to accept all points of views. You have to work with the likes of Ramesh, who will be competing with you all the time and others who want to usurp you and those who want to help you, and you have to be bias free. Can you do that?"

"OK. I will advise Andy, but it is his call."

"Srinivas, now don't get me wrong. This kind of infighting will get us nowhere."

"Why not advise the same to Ramesh?"

"I will. We will have a joint meeting. Just get the response corrected, and we will do something about it"

Avial for dinner

~~~~~~

“What is troubling you?” Malar asked Mani, turning off the grinder. The coconut paste was about right. The vegetables were in the pan with some water. She had measured each of the vegetables with her digital weigh scale and put the right proportion of vegetables in the Avial. She had to add the paste and stir it a couple of times. Then 'Done'!

"Oh nothing, except that everything hangs on one system, and that is not ready."

"Tell me about it." They had a large dining area, and the modern design of their apartment had the hall, kitchen and dining in one combined area. Mani liked to watch TV, sitting in the dining chairs and having a drink on weekend evenings. This weekday stuff was not normal, but happened when he was tense.

She had cut some carrots, cucumbers and added some kabuli chana sundal (boiled Chick-Pea, light fried and tossed with some spices) to make that evening's accompaniments. He ate a lot when he drank.

"There are many chemical processes or methods in layman terms to make a particular chemical product. This is similar to cooking a soup or making a burger with more complexities.

And just as in cooking, the recipe and the method defines or differentiates between products, the proportions, temperatures, and time, etc. define the product. In chemical and petrochemical plants, there is also a factor of economics to be considered.

Now in our plant, we have a reactor where a reaction occurs.

Many monomer, polymer and petrochemical processes have a mixture that acts as an activator of a reaction and many mixes that act as catalyst."

"I know. You told me last time, like I put curd into milk to convert the milk into curd . . . overnight."

"These different mixes have different purposes, some could start a reaction and keep it alive, and some could accelerate the reaction while some are required to have the reaction occur in the first place. And once the reaction has happened, these mixes have to be removed.

Just as an expert cook, making a curry, has to put the different spices in the proportionate correct quantity every time, so, in the industrial processes it is necessary to have the right quantities of the individual components. Each of these are measured by different instruments.

You could be weighing some components like 50 grams of spices. Now in an industry, you could be measuring 1000 or 100000 kgs at a time. When you weigh this much, your weigh scale could itself be wrong by a few kilos.

Or you could be measuring by volume, like two tea spoons of oil. In Industries, you could be measuring the level in a vessel, which itself could be wrong by a small percentage.

Or you could be pouring 100 ml over a period of time in your recipe. In industries, this rate of flow is measured as volume per time and totalized or calculated as to how much has flowed until then."

"Like I have weighed the vegetables that go into my Avial and measured every ingredient that goes into the gravy"

They had a small weighing scale where she weighed the vegetables as per the recipe. Over a period of time, she had accumulated different measuring spoons and small vessels for measuring up-to a liter or two. Mani insisted that she mix everything proportionately. She had developed this habit of using weigh scales, volumetric measurements and stuff like that since her marriage and was the envy of some of her relatives.

Some of the kids in the family had nicknamed her "Measurement Mami". (Measurement Maternal Aunt).

One time, she had to make dinner for 12 people and was skeptical. She had never made avail on this scale. Mani had then taken her recipe book and taught her to calculate new proportions. 100gms for 2 people became 600 gms for 12 and so on. With the weighing scales and measures that they had, each dish had come out perfect.

"Doing this day in and day out in an industry demands a consistency that few companies across the globe can offer.

So the first thing is to mix the right quantities to form the correct mixture and then to put the same at the correct time inside a cooking pot or a reactor in a chemical plant is very critical.

If you put in too much of the other ingredient, not only are you incurring more cost when making the mixture, but you are also making more unnecessary by-products, and you are incurring more money to remove the activators and catalysts and for removing by-products from the main product."

"See the same is true for my Avial. Sometimes the brinjals (eggplants) are small, sometimes long and so is the case with every vegetable. But I use your method of weighing in proportion and get the perfect recipe all the time. So what is the problem?"

"Now, simple as it sounds, you have three persons working in a day on the same, and they may have a fourth and fifth reliever so that these three people can have some holidays.

So four people have their individual way of interpreting and operating the controls."

Malar knew all about this. When 4 ladies got together to make a dish, everyone had to show off their skills.

"Like the Pongal in our native place?"

That got them laughing. They had been to their native place, and four women were in the garden making Pongal and how those four had argued, and the pongal had over cooked and some of it had been burnt. And all the families gathered in for their holidays had commented on how four women could not get one-dish right . . . .

"That's where the feed mix automator comes in. First, it provides the most exact mixture in the industry. And based upon the process condition, the recipe of the mixture could be changed. We have the expertise in that . . .

Here, The Austin group excels in providing the batch and mixing in the correct proportion, while, our company excels in changing the recipe based upon the process conditions."

"I still don't see why such experts as you have cannot make a good avial."

"The automator is too big in this new plant. And we had sent some boys to see the site, and they did not see that the space was too less. So we are looking for a solution and not finding any."

"Why don't you tell Srinivas. He will find a solution. Look when we had this space problem in the kitchen during your office party, . . . do you remember."

"Which office party?"

"When Sundar (their son) had got admission to engineering"

"Hunh . . . Yes."

She knew this expression. This meant that he did not recollect or was just saying 'yes' to proceed ahead. He would be turning the news channel on.

"The time when we had got twenty liters of coke and there was no place on the table, and he had kept that small stool and the big dispenser on it, and we could keep everything below that . . . ."

Malathy and Malar were friends and close confidants.

"You know what Srinivas has been up-to now. He has been visiting some Dance bars in America during office time, and I had to take action against some boy who influenced by him, has been neglecting work!"

"What! Srinivas going to dance bars! Malathy would be heartbroken." She needed to remind Malathy to keep a tight leash on her husband.

Mani was already a bit drunk. She had better make the 'Avial' real fast. He had already turned on the news channel.

She should have taken engineering. She was good at making Avial. Maybe, if she had taken engineering in college instead of BCom, she would have been able to help him now.

Men were anyways not good at making mixtures and Avials and things like that.

And who was this boy who was in such big trouble?

BOOK TWO

Prologue . . . Sort of . . . of the Game changing powder . . .

———❦———

I f you knew that the clothes that you wore, were made from a white powder mixed with a liquid, and imagined all the hazards in the processes, you would probably appreciate that piece of cloth a bit more!

Purified Terepthalic Acid or PTA is a powder that is used to produce polyester fibers, yarns. And Polyester is used to make clothes, furniture, upholstery, containers, films and many other products.

The PTA plant introduced in India in the 1980's was the game changer and challenged existing fiber producers who used DiMethyl Terepthalate or DMT. The cost of producing fiber from this route was more expensive and therefore, the plants with PTA won out. There could have been other strategic reasons for the same. However, that's what popular reading says.

The process of making PTA has its complexities. The oxidation reaction that produces the basic material that is further processed into making the powder occurs in a highly corrosive environment and highly exothermic reaction (or a reaction that produces a lot of heat). There is very less oxygen in the reactor and a high or a low concentration would mean that the process needs to be stopped.

In addition, the process is highly corrosive requiring exotic alloys and materials be used in pipelines and devices in contact with the chemicals.

In the first stage, the product is called Crude Terepthalic acid, which is dried and formed to a powder.

Then once again it is made into a slurry using water as solvent, for further improving the purity through various processes.

Then there is the use of hydrogen in the further stages of hydrogenation. Many people would relate hydrogen to hydrogen bombs. To say the least, there is a complexity here.

Once you have a powder, then the powder has to be transported. This transportation happens in pipelines, while liquids like water can be transported by pipelines very easily, the transmission of powder requires a fluid media to carry it in a pipe and at any point of time, there is a possibility of choking the line.

There are many complexities that require complex measurements and complex methods of controlling. You have to measure huge quantities of powder being filed into bags, or transferred through pipelines. The color of the powder is crucial and what not.

There are many manufacturers of PTA in the world.

The complexity of the process requires that they be controlled using the most advanced control systems. Each plant has an advanced control system and technology that is protected and patented. Many plants spread across continents are owned by huge business conglomerates.

With the prolific use of the Internet, many had thought that remote controls would be easily possible. But the threat of cyber attacks prevented systems from getting connected to the Internet.

Some developments are game changers in the industry. When ISA developed ISA 99 standard for cyber security, it ensured that the industry had a robust infrastructure that would allow remote control in a protected environment. ISA is the International Society of Automation.

Further, more technical advancements and developments allowed the operation and control of plants from across the globe. Soon it was realized that the chemical process plants could be controlled effectively from giant remote control rooms. A business giant could consolidate all the plants from its many manufacturing locations and control from one location.

This was highly cost-effective and in addition, operators could be in an urban environment. Operators loved this as did their families.

While on one hand, companies could consolidate their expertise in PTA plant control into one place. Efficiencies went up like anything. Their control center was like the 'Nalanda' or 'Taxashila' (Ancient Universities of knowledge in India) of PTA. New innovations and new operational strategies seemed to come out every day. There was a period of explosive innovation. Operating efficiencies increased every quarter. The application of best practices from one plant to another gave fantastic results.

The weakness of the rupee and the established remote methods of working in BFSI, Engineering and other industries, saw the setup of emote operating centers in India.

Traditional manufacturing companies that had this expertise and BFSI giants with their deep pockets competed for a piece of the remote operation's pie.

After having 43 PTA plant controls in a remote location, the Petrochem company was going on for shifting the control room operations of a 44th PTA plant located somewhere in the African continent to Ghansoli in India.

Everyone wants to corner the remote operations pie. The business is tough, it is going to give me a heart attack some day, Mani thought.

You had to keep an eye on the developments within the industry. Keep your secrets with you, try to retain the people working for you and above all answer, the MD!

His phone rang. It was the MD.

"Hi Mani. Good Morning."

"Good Morning Sir."

"What's going on Mani?"

"Sir, there are a few issues with the Operator Training Simulator. And as I reported there is some problem with the Automator."

"Mani, I am referring to the ethics complaint."

"Sir, it is just a misunderstanding. The two persons have been at odds because, one of them got to go to USA, and the other did not."

"Srinivas, Andy and Singh had gone . . . na."

"Yes sir. And Andy was responsible for the OTS."

"Somehow I felt that the complaint was more about Srinivas."

"The complaint specifically targets the OTS. And Andy was responsible for it. If you remember sir, we actually overloaded Srinivas with activities. He met and exceeded all targets. If it were against Srinivas, I would have thrown it out of the window immediately. He achieved the entire set of targets and then some more."

"Are our boys spending time in dance bars?"

"Sir, boys will be boys. We can only overload them with activity. What they do in their free time is their business"

"We need to be more careful in selecting people next time."

"Sir, you know Srinivas. He is a genius, and we cannot entrust some tasks to anyone else. He is the perfect candidate for any new task. He will quickly identify any lacunae, any new problems, hidden threats, new potentials and all. But he has his bad habits."

"I heard that he is lost too much into 'vasanas'." (Innuendo for sexual tendencies)

"Yes that is true. He is said to have got some furniture specifically meant for pleasure."

"How do you know?"

"His wife told my wife. You know women."

"Mani, I am worried that this one person, the one who wrote the complaint, did not tell anything to you, but wrote a complaint in the ethics portal."

"Sir, I will ask him why he did that."

"Mani, as top management we need to be more impartial than others. Are people viewing your proximity to Srinivas as a threat and feel that they cannot get a balanced . . . hmnnn judgment . . . . approach"?

"Sir, the person reports to Ramesh. Sir, do you remember, we had discussed this approach of competing teams may have some fallbacks. Since the team that we selected went to USA, the other team has been feeling been left out. This is finally a result of that competitiveness."

"The complaint says that the OTS is not working."

"Yes Sir. But Srinivas says that it is working, and we had done a couple of remote sessions and seen most of the working software." This memory had come as Mani was speaking to the MD. "Sir, it is some kind of backup or wrong software loaded issue."

Why did he not recollect this earlier? Of course, they had remote tested the OTS, and it was working.

"Are you sure? I do not want to question your authority. I know that if you say you have seen it working, then it is working."

"I will get to the bottom of this and solve it."

"No Mani. Leave it to the team to solve. You need to get the team spirit back. Mani, you have to see the results of past decisions and keep correcting the course. That's why you get the top dollar. I am not very happy with this. If I just want reports and postmortem analysis, I can get a dozen graduates to do that. Mani, you have to understand your role."

"OK sir I will take necessary steps to get this resolved."

"I'll be in touch and let's see if you need some help."

"Sir, give me a couple of days on this. Else I'll myself ask for help."

"Mani, I trust you. But keep me posted on the developments."

"Yes sir."

Mani took some deep breaths after the call.

Had his team moved far away from him?

He needed to analyze if his team believed he was impartial or did they feel he was playing favorites?

He had kept close tabs and knew the rifts created by part of the team going to USA.

He thought for some more time on the next course of Action.

Sleeping with the enemy

Mani felt something bothering him, about the feed mix automator. What was it? When did this nagging feeling start? Since Malar had served him Avial. What would be so complex about it? Why could his people not solve this one simple issue?

Nincompoops! All of his people. All of them. Why could they not come upon a solution without him intervening? When will he be able to comfortably hand over the reins to Haresh? Will Ramesh and Srinivas be ready to take over building one and two on their own?

He had to don the hat of engineer and think of solutions or guide these men like cowherd steering cows!

He knew that without the automator, the processing costs would be higher, and he would have to keep a few operators at the site. And quality would be a concern.

The MD would not be happy.

What else could he have done?

It had always been a top priority for him.

He had approved the request from Andy. Sent those 'bunch of jokers' that the vendor calls engineers to site. I cannot be omnipresent like Vishnu! His BP was rising. He closed his eyes and took a few deep breaths.

The extra expense was worth if the automator had worked smoothly. Now he was left with a non working automator and had to also explain the extra expense. But those engineers had also faced a tough time at site.

That young chap Andy needed some grooming. He should be result oriented. What he was getting was excuses . . . Be tough on the vendors. Make them earn their buck. And also be friendly . . . or businesslike . . . These young chaps get so confused between business relationships and friendly personal relationships.

He was afraid of how much more grilling he had to go through on account of this Automator. The MD could be harsh and cruel at times. That had the effect of driving senior people to achieve their goals.

First things first, he had to first put his house in order. Get his team motivated to work as one. Remove the discord in the team. The MD was certain to send someone around. He had better fix this issue before all that happened.

What should he do now?

Get the warring factions together and start them moving forward towards their goal of getting PTA44 running.

He quickly needed to call an emergency meeting. Get some tea and biscuits, rather get some cold drinks. He wanted a more relaxed atmosphere. He placed a call to his secretary and asked to organize everything.

He arrived a good three minutes late. He looked around the room. Get the people know all in the room. Maybe the biscuits and cold drinks would bring in some camaraderie.

Last night seemed to be heavy on all of them.

Andy looked haggard, as if he had not slept the whole night. Srinivas was lost in thought as were Ramesh and Subba. Good, he needed them in a conducive state of mind, where he could drive his point easily!

"OK guys let's start. I am deeply disappointed at the way this thing is moving forward.

Let us start one by one. What is the chief Concern?

People going abroad and wasting company money, etc. etc."

"Sir . . ." Andy started but Mani cut him off.

"Everybody will get a chance to have their say."

Ramesh started "Sir, for PTA44 project we had sent a team of three persons to USA for the operator training simulator or OTS. The task was supposed to be simple.

Convert the PTA 12 training software . . . . It was to be slightly modified to make it suitable for PTA44. Now the team was supposed to go for two weeks and fix everything. However, they extended their stay to six weeks."

"Ramesh, I know all this. I approved the extension."

"Well it seems that the team did nothing in USA but go to clubs and shop and return. In fact, senior members are supposed to have attended meetings from clubs."

"What's your problem Ramesh?" Srinivas started. "All your accusations are wrong. The key member on the team for OTS, was Andy and nobody here can question his sincerity. I will personally vouch that he worked day in and day out, and I had to drag him from work at times." Then addressing Mani, "Sir, these accusations happen all the time, especially when anyone goes abroad to the west. Andy is our sincere-most employee, and I will not tolerate anything said against him.

Those who are accusing us of wrong doing should at least be clean. We know what you guys are doing when you go out for trips here."

Srinivas was now glaring at Subba and Ramesh.

Mani intervened ""Stop this Gang-war behavior immediately!"" He said at the top of his voice. The team gathered there had never heard his raised voice and could not believe that he could be so authoritative.

"Looks like all of you are taking the company for a ride. This will not do! Ramesh! Is there truth in these counter allegations?"

"No Sir! That is absolute rubbish! Whenever we visit the Vendor's, we all come early to work and as the vendor closes early, people get to go home earlier. But we ensure that they put in the required time."

"OK, so you and Srinivas are saying that all accusations on each other are wrong." Mani summarized "So please keep to facts and do not accuse each other of things." Mani continued at a lower voice.

"Sir," Ramesh started, "The software is not suitable for PTA44. It seems that only the title was changed to PTA44 and our team was there. I am not blaming Andy. He is having less experience with these Americans. Senior person like Srinivas was supposed to manage the Americans and get the work done."

Srinivas almost got up from the table, but Mani motioned him to stop.

"I will ask Andy, to speak up if he faced any difficulty and why the software is not working."

"First, sir, I would like to clear that we worked very hard in USA. Every bug, every change was attended to. Looks like the software backup taken had some issues. We will load another copy, and everything will be all right."

Ramesh would not give up "Andy you must come clear on all these rumors about the team and what happened in USA."

"Go on Andy, If you have any concern, speak up." Mani encouraged.

He was a good judge of people and knew that Andy would not say anything against Srinivas.

"Sir, I can only answer for my domain of activity. The training system software was my responsibility. Singh and Srinivas were to perform the tests. They had a lesser role to play . . . . time wise. Srinivas pointed all the bugs, and we fixed them. Now after office hours, it is their personal life. I do not wish to make any comment on that."

"I agree with Andy. Look guys, we do not want to get carried away. What an individual does after office hours is their business.

If you all remember, we had three remote sessions with the Training software. Ramesh and Subba were not involved in those tests as the reliever team had done that. I had just touched base with them in the past and had forgotten about it when the accusations against the OTS came in. I called and asked them today and they too vouch that the training system was working. I think, as Andy has said, this seems to be a case of loading the wrong software.

Further, the MD called me today morning. He is extremely disappointed at us for not being team players.

This is not the time to point fingers at each other.

If there is anything wrong, let us work together to fix it.

Let me ask you one question." He paused for some effect. The mention of the MD sobered the team even further. The cold drinks had arrived by that time.

He motioned everyone to have their drink.

"I have seen Andy work very hard and in these four years, we have come to rely on him to deliver results. He has put in very long hours, and he has never failed us. Do you all believe in Andy?"

The room echoed with "Yes's. They all liked and trusted Andy.

"I want all of us to work together to help Andy resolve these issues. This is no longer Andy's issue alone, but this problem is our problem." He burped. There was some laughter in the room. He also laughed a bit.

"And Andy, get the reply to Showcause ready. I have already directed Srinivas on the way the reply has to be drafted.

I know many of you wanted to be part of the team and be a part of the effort to get the training software right in Austin. I would have let all of you go to Austin, if it was possible.

But our business demands that we be frugal and only the minimum number of people travel.

But, if you have seen the history of our company, everyone gets to travel. So you all will get your chances.

I know that sometimes when we are working, we create competing forces in our industry. But this competition is only to help us shape up better. Not to get us fighting over small issues.

Ramesh, Srinivas, both of you used to go, hand on each other's shoulders a few years back.

You two need to think and ask yourselves 'What has changed?'" This emotional note got everyone silent.

"Believe me guys, to the management, we are one unit. The comparison is between building one and two teams. However, building one is one team.

Which team is performing well?

Which team has the skill set?

It is always building one as one unit or team and building two as another.

Believe me if anyone of you loses, we all lose.

The team loses. Building two loses.

This will put a blemish on all of us.

I urge all of you to keep the team spirit up."

The team clapped at his speech.

However, he was not finished yet.

"As you all know, the feed mix automator is not ready." This was a pain point and needed to be addressed. "There would be a lot of complaints as the quality would be affected, and the operators would be pointing fingers at each other.

And it may be so for some time." There was some murmur in the room.

"We need a contingency plan."

Srinivas quickly added. "That's not so big an issue. I mean that's not a show stopper. We can do the feed mix operation manually."

Ramesh chipped in "But Srinivas, with that, all the batches would come in haywire."

"No Ramesh, do you remember that I had made the feedmix logic with smaller batches. For the scenario where the automator fails."

"Ohhh Yes. But as I told you, it needs a more elaborate procedure."

"Why (do we need) procedure for this simple thing.

We had this problem in the automator in PTA15, and we worked those days in 12-hour shifts. We also made a feedback logic wherein we adjusted the other rates to get the production going. And we would keep correcting the feedmix in small batches. This got us to a very accurate feedmix."

"Srinivas, that was because we were doing it together and knew all the undocumented aspects. If you hand it over to operators, it will be too many different people. A procedure is needed."

"OK Ramesh, then you have to make one." Mani intervened "OK now explain this system in brief."

Srinivas quickly explained the system that they had created.

Mani realized that these two together were a formidable team.

"Good idea Srinivas. Ramesh, get the procedure for doing this ready by evening. And team, remember, that this is a stop-gap arrangement. We need the automator working in a short while."

Hush Hush Business

———❧❦❧———

It was a long day after a long evening. Everything had turned out so different, so against everybody's expectations. Last night, Andy had hardly slept. He was awake within three hours and drove early to office.

First things first . . . Get the Training system in order.

He opened his desk and got the final copy of the training software. He loaded the DVD backup into his laptop and quickly opened the folder that contained the software. The date matched the last day in Austin.

He quickly opened the file in notepad.

Most users needed to load the software into the training system environment software. The system had checks and balances that prevented loading into any system and required specific licenses. However, you could open in notepad and see a long list of commands, codes and elements that would not make sense to most engineers.

However, Andy was no novice. He was one of the experts who could build the entire software in notepad. He looked at the various descriptors.

They all said 'PTA12'!

Oh My God! He whispered.

Somebody who had taken the backup, had backed up the wrong set of files.

So Subba's grouse was correct. They had indeed screwed up.

He should have checked earlier.

He dialed Marshall's number in USA.

"Cahill here."

"Hi Marshall, we have loaded the software, but it is all the original PTA12 software."

"Can't be! We had sure asked the server team to give us the latest backup."

Modern computer systems have a DVD or CD writer of their own. However, confidentiality agreements needed that people not be able to take backups. Secrets had to be preserved! So all the DVD and CD drives were disabled.

Even USB drives in all computers were blocked out.

Their business was 50 years old and had a process that was described in the Internet, yet there were many components that were company secrets.

An elaborate procedure was formulated that required that only the IT department could provide backup, and that was possible only after several authorizations were signed.

So the entire software was stored on a server, and nobody was allowed on the premises with a hard-disk, USB memory device or CD—DVD drives. Taking data out of the server was impossible for an ordinary person.

So the team had put up the request and found that the IT in-charge and his relievers were on holiday, and so the backup would be available on the last working day.

The backup was finally handed over just as the team was leaving for India.

"Just in time." they had joked on that day.

Andy gave up all hope. It was Murphy's law at play.

Everything that could go wrong did.

"Let me check." Marshall offered. "Give me an hour."

"OK. Thanks."

So Andy had left for the meeting that Mani had called. It was early in India and late in USA. The IT guys in USA would have left for the day. So Marshall would have to go to the server and get the backup.

The realization that the team that had gone to USA was at fault had made Andy less belligerent. He was thinking of options when he had gone to the emergency meeting. Subba's complaint had some merit, though Andy felt that Andy was not at fault.

That was why Andy was very amicable to redrafting the letter.

When Andy came back from the meeting, he saw a missed call from Austin. He surmised that it must have been Marshall Cahill.

He dialed the number.

"Hi Marshall. Any good news."

"Yes. The software on the server is the old software. I checked with the server team here. We had had a system outage the evening before you left and everything from the server loads on its own, but your confidentiality agreement required that your software be manually loaded by your team. Looks like an older original training software got loaded."

Cahill continued. "But they have an image that would have our software. They will load this image and then we will get our software. This may take a couple of days.

I will send you the software by our file transfer system."

Andy did not want to wait for two days. That would take away the faith from the Austin system suppliers even more.

But he had no choice.

Srinivas came in.

"Hey Andy, good letter. Aisa kuch maloom hoga to mereko bhi batate rehna. Nahin to saala log sar pe chad jaayega." (if you know of some such things, let me know, else these people will sit on our head.).

"No Srinivas, the backup that we had taken was wrong. I do not know how, but the backup is still the old software."

"You mean the backup that we took from Austin."

"Yes, you remember that they had an outage, and we got the copies late

The entire system gets automatically recovered, but we had to manually load our training software. Looks like the original software got loaded. Our software being the 'Hush Hush' one!

So we have to wait for another two days."

Srinivas looked unperturbed. 'Que Sera Sera . . . whatever will be will be!"

Srinivas took out his mobile. "Do you have your cable?"

Andy had a multi-purpose charger cable. Srinivas had in the past, borrowed Andy's cable and charged his mobile from the computer's USB port.

"Kya, phir dishcharge ho gaya?" Andy questioned him (has it got discharged again.)

Srinivas had a mischievous smile.

Andy handed over the cable.

Srinivas connected and put his mobile in USB storage mode.

Andy could see a bunch of folders.

Was Srinivas going to show him some porn clips again? This was not the time.

He knew that Srinivas's mobile was a treasure trove of carnal knowledge.

"Srinivas, this is really not the time. I'm in no mood."

"When you see this you will get recharged."

Andy felt exasperated. This guy was really a sex maniac. What clip did he have that could recharge him.

"See my magic now." Saying so, he opened a folder.

Andy could not believe it.

In that folder was a daily backup of their training software.

"Srinivas, you are a life saver!"

"Vatsa! Humne kaha tha tum recharge ho jaaoge!" Srinivas mimicked the style from the TV serial Mahabharat. (So I said that you will get recharged.)

"Dhanya Ho taatshree . . . Dhanya ho!" (blessed be you Grandfather great grandfather) Andy replied mimicking the characters in Mahabharat. "But how did you manage this. All the USB ports were locked."

"The engineering station had three USB ports while the others had two. I once tried the third port and saw that it was enabled. I took regular backups of the software."

"Oh great." Andy thought that he should quickly load it to the training server.

"OK, I think you would like to load the software now. I will go for some tea."

Andy literally ran to the training room.

Luckily, it was tea break, so there was no one in the training room. He quickly loaded the software and tested a few routines.

Everything was OK! What luck!

Srinivas had saved the day for him.

Subba came in and raised his hand apologetically.

"Sorry boss, it was not against you. However, it backfired."

"I know. It's ok. The training software is now working."

However, Subba did not leave him at that. Andy had to test all the routines with him.

By the time it was done, it was almost 8 PM.

Mani caught him as he started to go into his cabin.

"Hey Andy, you did not turn in the reply."

Andy beamed and replied that the training software was working.

"You mean that there was some minor glitch."

"No sir, the server in Austin was down the evening prior to one, when we had left for India. So somehow the old software got copied into the backup CD. Luckily Srinivas had a copy, and that was the latest."

"So Srinivas has saved the day for you."

"Yes sir."

"OK. But don't forget to provide a logical explanation to the issue.'

"Yes sir."

"And Andy No 'pointing fingers' at anyone, please. Keep it objective."

"Yes sir."

1% inspiration and 99% perspiration

Mani did not expect Srinivas to wait until late in the evening. He loved to leave by 5:30 PM in the evening.

What did he do after going home?

Mani knew that he never sat with his children and guided their studies. In fact, he was blessed to have two intelligent sons who continuously topped their class. The children, it seemed studied on their own. He had asked Srinivas, what he did once he got home.

Srinivas read a lot, and he could be interested in one subject today and another one a few weeks down the line.

He had gone crazy after organic farming once and did some earthworm farming at home. This happened until

Malathy got fed up with all the dirt and donated the entire thing to a farmer.

Or once he became interested in a fish tank and spent a fortune in making a fish tank at home.

The kids loved their irresponsible father, and much of the disciplining was left to Malathy.

And of course, his knowledge on sex was tremendous. Mani was quite close to Srinivas, and once he got Srinivas in the mood, Mani was sure that Srinivas would have some new technique to divulge.

"What happened to the furniture you got from America."

That got him talking about this "Scoop" thing.

"What's this 'scoop'?"

So Srinivas explained the rocking motion pillow.

"You mean it is like a rocking chair or the "oonjal" (a kind of big swing that used to be in homes in ancient India) that we used to have in the past?"

"No, for that, they have body swings and sex swings. This is more like a rocking bed."

"It seems that it is for teenagers. Is it safe?"

"Yes. In USA, even 70-year-old people use it." Srinivas exaggerated.

"I should get one for myself."

"Hey, I got two in this trip. I will give you one."

"How much does it cost?"

"200 $ after discount."

"Oh! That is expensive. Thirteen thousand rupees. More than my first year's entire salary!" Mani referred often to the paltry salary of one thousand rupees he received every month at the beginning of his career.

"Yes, it seems expensive, but the experience is fantastic."

"It looks like an opportunity to manufacture in China and sell to the world."

"Why did you get two?"

Srinivas started on his theory of tying the two together and explained the various motions possible. Mani smiled at the enthusiasm in Srinivas's eyes. He was so childish and innocent.

Suddenly, the phone rang. It was the MD. Mani quickly informed that they were on speaker phone and Srinivas was there. After the informal Hi's.

"Mani, how has this ethics thing 'panned out'."

"Sir, turned out that the backup processes at the vendor had some issue, and we got the wrong backup. But luckily, we had another good backup, and things were restored."

"So the complaint was a waste."

"Yes sir. They (Subba) want to take it out of the system."

"That is not as critical as having the training system working and knowing that the integrity of our staff is intact."

"They are all virgins. Our people are very hardworking."

"And Srinivas, How are your children doing in school?"

"Oh sir, both of them are doing well."

"I keep hearing that they do extremely well at school and do our school proud. Congratulate them. Keep their spirits up."

Srinivas felt pride in his children's achievements like never before.

"And what is this, I hear you got furniture from USA? I always thought that everything in USA is made in our neighboring country, China."

'Sir, it is some special furniture that he has bought for his wife."

They all laughed at this.

"And what happened to the feed mix automator"

Mani explained the contingency plan.

"Good thinking Srinivas and Mani. But look for alternatives to this issue. This step is OK for testing and test batch runs, but before we go for full-fledged production, I want the automator running."

"Yes Sir."

"And Srinivas, one day, you will be leading a team. You should be careful, what you do and what you do not do. Where you go and what you do will be important. You do not want to set up a wrong example for others. Think about this."

"Yes Sir. I will keep that in Mind." Srinivas answered.

The MD thanked them and hung up.

Mani again felt something about the Feed mix bothering him, but he could not put a finger on to it. What was it?

"Let's go to Ramesh's room and see the procedure."

"OK"

Ramesh generally hated cleaning after someone's mess as much as any other person does. But today he was motivated by Mani's speech. He thought of days gone by, when he and Srinivas were one team and did wonders in the plant.

He looked at the SOP (Standard Operating Procedures) manual in front of him. The steps had to be written without assuming anything. The last time the SOP for manual operation was written as an after-thought, something that their operation process demanded. Nobody had imagined that it would ever get used. So the consultant had turned out a rudimentary process, which failed during first application. The operators found gaps in the procedure and tried to remember what to do from their past experience, and every operator did things differently.

The whole plant had a big problem and people pointing fingers at each other.

And to think that he and Srinivas used to do this without a procedure for months altogether!

He focused and analyzed each step of the process.

Slowly, he drew up a firm procedure based on what needed to be done. He did not leave even a micro-step out of the procedure. The operator could be a zombie and still could not do a mistake.

After he had done the first pass, he took each step and looked at all possible plant scenarios, plant failure scenarios and created alternatives where required.

He had started at around 10 in the morning and had lunch brought to his office. He had his 3PM tea in his office. He was just wrapping up when Srinivas and Mani entered the room.

"Hi Ramesh."

"Hi. I'm done. It finished just now!"

Srinivas and Mani looked at the procedure. It was a big document. Ramesh quickly explained that the operator needed just a cross-reference table and correct operating procedure to do the activity.

"Any ways let us put it in the DCS system so that operators can easily access it."

Mani was happy with the outcome.

They had the contingency plan working.

"Ramesh, Srinivas, something about the Automator is bothering me?"

"Ramesh, Srinivas shall we go through the drawing?"

Ramesh opened the drawing.

"This is the right wall, and these are the two beams. If we superimpose the feed automator, there is no place." Ramesh said.

"Sir, I have checked many times, but there is no space where we can squeeze it." Srinivas added.

"Hmnnn . . . Something is bothering me from last night, but I am unable to put my finger on to it."

"How about the contract . . . No . . . We have gone through it twice . . . The Americans are very clear in their contract. Even the trip their people made came without strings attached to it."

"The space requirement was there from the beginning.

"OK. I think we have to take a break. Let's call it a day."

Bonsai Automator . . .

Cahill looked at the request from Jerry. The Automator size was to be reduced. He called it 'The Bonsai Automator' Project.

Sometimes he felt that people were losing out on the romance of developing a new product. Someone discovered radioactivity and after more than a century, you had a nuclear bomb. Nowadays, it seems that an invention happens and the next one follows it with such speed that it seemed like a parallel development.

As Andy had said, there was a time when a song became a hit and then ages later you had a remix come out. However, nowadays the remix and the original song are part of the same album.

The process of a company selecting a technology and promoting it is complex and has its threats. First, there is a pool of ideas. His company had one such vast pool of ideas.

Some of them were too unrealistic or far-fetched that they may not see the light of day. And many where the benefits seemed almost identical to the other choice. They could obviously not implement all the ideas. That would require an amount that was unimaginable.

Technology was not the sole criteria for selecting a technology. Generally, Business need, ease of making and cost of making it seemed more important drivers. Sometimes an idea that they had originally thrown out as impractical becomes the need of the hour.

And at times, something is discarded and the competition implements such an idea that is hugely successful.

When they had zoomed into the concept of a Feed-Mix Automator, for plants where powders, liquids and slurries had to be proportionately mixed and at the same time analyzed, it had seemed a far-fetched concept. Lying in that pool of ideas, gathering cosmic dust.

Then one day, they had faced the problems in the Indian company's PTA plant. Two heads of business units meet, and small talk and then this issue is discussed.

'Say, you are in this Automation business, and we have this problem with our feed mix that needs automation.'

'Consider it solved.' Say's the CEO.

And when the CEO entrusted the activity to Cahill and asked him what they had on it, it was by chance that he had stumbled onto this idea.

He decided to dive into the past pool of ideas and when he looked at the pool, he realized that the pool had over time become an ocean. He felt that an effort be made to catalogue the ideas. Maybe some ideas were overlapping and some that were proved incorrect by other competitors. Well, as they say, luck favors the bold . . . So he looked at this idea that had a lot of mechanical engineering to be done.

The Author had briefly described that the different technologies using flowmeters, totalizers, level based measurements, analyzers and technologies that they had from dealing with powders and slurries be mixed to create a unique product called the Feed Mix Automator.

Cahill got the best heads involved in creating a concept document. Some brief cost analysis was done, and they got Jerry to manage the project.

And so they had made the first Automator in collaboration with their Innovation center and a fabricator in Korea. But the Indian company wanted to be involved from the initial stages.

During the fabrication, Srinivas who had been a key driver for the Automator's selection among many technologies from other vendor companies, had made many changes. The people in Austin had developed a respect for Srinivas and his ideas.

Ramesh had been frustrated at the poor documentation standards of the Korean's. The Austin personnel realized that the client's personnel were very diligent and demanded the highest standards of documentation. Cahill was used to such teething problems. When two communities come together for the first time, they Form, Storm, Norm and Perform. The Koreans would get adjusted to the Indian company's needs over time.

"The revision history is a mess. We do not know at times which the initial design document is and which one is the last. And they do not mark any dimensions." He had literally wanted that the engineering be handed over to one of the EPC giants in India. But somehow the Korean company persisted and exceeded Ramesh's expectations. Koreans have that tenacity!

Now Mani's call and request were disturbing because Jerry had already touched base with him earlier. That meant that these requests were being routed through multiple channels. He knew the Indian petrochemical company's ways. He guessed that already, twenty to thirty top notch professionals were analyzing the Automator and tearing apart the design.

When Cahill's multinational company provided a design, he did not want the Indian petrochemical company's engineers to discard parts of it, or suggest improvements. That had a risk of delaying the project.

Mani, on the other hand, though happy at the outcome of the progress made during the day, did not want to leave the Automator aside.

Yes, his team was motivated.

They trusted him.

And the training software was working.

The procedure for operating feed mix manually was robust and in place.

However, he should fix the Automator. That's what the MD had meant, when he said that he was paying Mani, top dollar to think ahead of the visible paths in front of them.

"Marshall, we need to reduce the size of the Automator."

"That's easier said than done."

"But it is possible right?"

"Yes Mani. It is possible. We have been discussing this for some time.

It requires us to redesign the placement of the different components and maybe look into the methods on how the maintenance teams will work with the changed orientation.

Preliminary thoughts that our team had, indicate that the design may take up-to eight weeks to materialize. This is without any comments from your side on the final engineering documents."

"What if I were to embed Ramesh and Srinivas in the design teams. I suppose that would be in Austin."

Cahill disliked having the client's team involved from the initial stages.

Sometimes, the thoughts and concepts seem to get hijacked to the other organization. However, he knew that it was better to work together on this one. This was a high-risk game. Having the client onboard would stop any incriminations at a later stage.

"Well that's where the surprise element comes into play. The Koreans are too busy for a couple if exhibitions that are to happen in Korea. Marine industry exhibition followed by the petrochemical one in Seoul and Busan. So this may have to be done in Korea now."

"Korea? Well OK. In fact, that reduces the travel time for us."

"But it increases the cost for us. It is better to wait until these exhibitions are over and follow the earlier route. That way costs would be minimal."

"Marshall, what you say is that time-wise, the earliest possibility is eight weeks of design and eight weeks of fabrication. So in 16 weeks we have the smaller-sized Automator." Mani wanted to wrap this up quickly.

He had asked Malar to make muttacose kuttu (cabbage in a south Indian gravy) for dinner, and he was hungry now.

"Eight weeks was what the Koreans said on the phone. However, you know as with any new product development, the time could slip."

"Frankly, even the sixteen weeks are too much for us. We should be done with this faster. As it is they have the Automator fabricated. So this may only mean minor rearrangement."

"The schedule right now is sixteen weeks, and that's where it stays until we hear or find otherwise. And again, I know the time pressure on you, but product development takes time. You cannot have nine women making a baby in one month!" Cahill, knew that the way Asians typically liked to crash a schedule or reduce time to complete an activity or project was by throwing in many people. Yes, they had a quantity of engineers available at lower costs. But this did not work all the time.

Mani had heard this 'nine months for one woman and why nine women cannot deliver in one month' cliché, many times.

"Well Marshall, this baby needs to come out in less time. If a caesarean has to be done, then so be it and if the baby needs an incubator for some time, then that's that." He was already visualizing a scenario, where part of the fabrication may even happen at the site. In the past, he had made so many modifications and customizations when western suppliers had forgotten customization or the Indian way of working. Many times, by such acts, the entire equipment's warranty was voided. He had many a times risked, losing the warranty, provided for contingency and never once had he failed.

"Calculated risks have to be taken. Any ways, send me the details by Monday and let's see what can be done."

After the conversation, he sent an Email to the MD and marked it important. He did not want to have a long discussion. It was already quite late in the evening.

But no sooner had he sent the email, the phone rang.

It was the MD.

"Yes Mani."

"There is a possibility of a smaller Automator."

"I guessed so. However, the re engineering would be some effort."

"They say that it will take 16 weeks. And that is if it is expedited."

"That's too long."

"I gave them six weeks."

"What did they say?"

"The same old, 'Nine months one woman and not possible for nine women in one month' dialogue."

"Then?"

"I gave the Caesarean reply." They both laughed at that. The MD had invented that when one of the vendors had used this cliché a long time back. They used it but very rarely and judiciously.

"OK. Let's get the details. It is interesting, but I would have preferred no changes in schedule and cost."

"OK sir."

"And Mani, I think you need to move up your responsibilities. You will be dealing with the client on this. Do your best and take the correct direction. Keep me in the loop."

"Hmmnh . . . That's new water to tread for me."

"Don't worry. I will be there if you need me."

"OK."

"Good Night."

"Good Night sir."

A new perspective in life

$\sim\!\!\bullet\!\!\sim$

Jay had been impatiently waiting to get the news out of Andy. What had happened?

Did Aarti's family agree to their alliance?

Did they put any conditions?

The suspense was killing him!

This is what happened the last evening.

Aarti's home was within walk-able distance of the bus station or as people say 'ST stand'. (State Transportation Buses have a bus station, which is called ST stand). The ST stand in remote villages has the prominence equivalent to a metro station or suburban railway station in urban places.

Most often it is the center of town. You could trace the development taking root here and spreading around. This was generally a crowded place. And once the town developed substantially or could be called self-sustained, the other businesses wanted this central place, and the ST stand could be partially or completely moved to a new location.

Like all young lovers probably do, Aarti had, in the past, shown Andy her home from a distance. She had insisted that he follow her from the ST stand to her home. So Andy had done in the past. He knew the path to her home.

Andy parked the car near the ST stand. In fact, he got a place near the same sugarcane vendor like last time. He felt that this was a good omen. He started his march towards Aarti's home.

Aarti's mother opened the door and Aarti, who was just behind her, feigned surprise.

"Why have you come?" Her mother demanded.

"See all this is a mistake." Andy tried to articulate the words.

"Come in and talk." Aarti offered and her mother not wanting a scene for the neighbor's to watch, let Andy come in.

"Aarti, you go inside." her mother commanded.

"Aai (Mother), we are in this together. I will wait here." Andy's spirits started rising as he saw that fighting spirit in Aarti.

"Your tongue has grown long. We should have treated you harshly, like other families do to their girls."

Buy Aarti stood her ground.

India is Modern and so are Indian people. When their neighbor's son or daughter falls in love with someone from a different caste or community, they talk of secularism and neighborly love and cultural mix. However, when their own daughter's fall for someone from another community or region, they go back a 1000 years and become feudal, communal and orthodox.

Andy started." We were going to inform all of you 'properly' and seek your blessings. However, before we got a chance, all this happened."

"For how long has this been going on?"

"One and a half years" Aarti blurted out.

"And you find time now. Where are your parents? Ideally, they should have come here to ask for Aarti's hand in marriage."

"I will call them and inform." Andy informed.

What Andy did not know was that Aarti, Kiran and their mother had been up all night. Mother and son, probing and getting the details out of Aarti.

To add to the complication, Kiran knew some Sainiks from the small town where Andy had done his engineering.

The sordid details of Andy's affairs, incidents stretched beyond facts by people's imaginations, scared both the Mother and Son.

They were afraid that what Aarti took so seriously could just be a fling for Andy.

Sometimes a fear that one of Andy's old girlfriends would come into their lives and spoil her future terrified them, while at other times, they were afraid that he would be a drunkard or drug addict.

When they informed Aarti about Andy's past, she told that she already knew all these things that Andy had done in the past. But he had changed.

"What do you mean changed?" Kiran started

"How can you be sure?" Mother asking her now. "What if he changes again tomorrow?"

What if this girl enters his life again?

What if that girl did?

What if he turned into a womanizer later on?

Do you know that he also took drugs?

"That is bullshit!"

"How can you say that?"

"Andy told me."

"Aarti, do you realize that Andy may well have lied about all this. Nothing is lost. You have had an affair. But these things can be put behind

You are beautiful. There are a hundred boys in our community who will easily forgive you of this misbehavior and marry you."

"But I don't want to. I want to live my life with Andy. Why don't you understand?"

Then they got into reasons why she must have fallen in love with Andy.

"What has he promised you?"

"Are you lured by his car?"

"Has he lured you by saying that he will take you abroad. There are a thousand boys from our community who are living abroad. Just put your finger on the world map, and we will arrange an alliance with a boy from our community and living in that country."

"Are you lured by his education? He is a B.E. (Bachelor of Engineering), we will go for a M.E." (Masters in Engineering).

Aarti had become tired, answering many such questions and defending her position. They would never understand her love for Andy. It was love, pure intention-less love.

"Aarti, we understand that you love him. And your love is blind. Just trust us."

Then,

Do you trust us?

Trust us and don't marry this boy.

Trust us, this boy is not suitable for you.?

Trust us, He will not keep you happy.

Then finally groveling.

"Do this for the sake of your mother and brother."

"Do this because you love us."

And when they found her resolve not going down a bit, they became angrier.

He must have used some black magic. She does not listen to her own mother and brother.

People with whom she has spent a lifetime mean nothing to her today.

This boy from yesterday means so much more than your own blood!

Andy did not look like someone capable of black magic.

"Andy, you put yourself in our shoes. We started enquiring about you from yesterday, and we have heard so many bad things. It seems that there were so many girls in your life. Isn't it true that you promised marriage to so many girls?"

Andy was silent.

"Aai (Mother), I told you that he had told me all this."

"How does that change anything? He promised the ultimate to so many girls and did not turn up."

"I'm sorry about what I did during my college days. But I was very young and did not know exactly what to do. I made mistakes. But I am mature now and will not make these mistakes."

"You took drugs."

"That is not true. I have never taken drugs during my entire life. All these are rumors."

"Aai (mother) we have been through this the entire night. Enough! I trust him."

Kiran suddenly arrived out of nowhere. He had three or four strongmen with him.

The atmosphere looked hostile.

"Look I guarantee, that I will take care of Aarti for my entire life. As a small boy in college, I made some mistakes. But I love your daughter and will do anything for her. Just trust me."

Kiran suddenly asked, "Who proposed first? You or her."

Andy was surprised. How did this matter? What if he had done so and what if she had?

But in between drinks, one of his goon-friends Vishal had asked Kiran this question. "Who started this?"

"What do you mean by 'who started it'?"

"Did your sister propose or did he?"

"Of course he proposed!"

"How do you know? Did you ask?"

"Why should there be a need to ask?'

"You never know. My wife Shruti, well she was so docile, though she was the daughter of 'the Don' of our village. Her father asked this question, and she was the one who had proposed. That solved it all. Else, I would be dead now."

So it mattered to Kiran, If Andy had proposed, then he would bash him up. That would be alright.

So when Andy replied "How does that matter now?"

Kiran raised his voice and asked him again "Who proposed first?"

Aarti stepped in. "I did!"

That took the steam out of Kiran.

He turned back and punched the wall.

"Andy do you love me." Aarti asked again.

"Yes. Look I will call my father and do all this properly."

Aarti went in and brought Kumkum powder.

She handed this to Andy.

"Apply this to my forehead." She commanded in a loud voice.

Andy complied. Vishal and one goon friend had come in now.

"I am your wife now. I will leave with you now."

"Aarti, what is this madness?" Her mother demanded.

"Aarti, I know everyone is fed up with this stress. I want to get married to you in a proper function and start our married life. Just relax."

Aarti's mother was happy that Andy had the correct sensibility.

"No! Andy I will leave with you now. I will see that no girl enters your life, and none of the bad things happen. Either I go with you, or I die now!" She gave a surprise ultimatum.

Her mother hugged her and started crying. "Don't do this. Don't bring shame to our family."

"No. I will leave with him now. He is my choice.

I do not trust you. You could bring some new groom tomorrow." Suddenly, all the fears that they had tried to install in her last night were taking effect.

"Dada (elder brother) you go to Ahmedabad and meet his parents and fix everything for the marriage to show people."

She gripped Andy's hand and said, "Let's go now."

The three of them looked at her. She looked a very different person.

"Aarti, nobody will do anything to you. I will talk with my father and fix everything very fast." Andy tried to soothe her.

"Aarti, you win. We will get you married to Andy. If that is your choice." Both mother and son promised.

"Ha ha ha." Aarti mocked a laugh. "Last night, you were saying the exact opposite. I will not leave him. I will go now."

Everyone was getting scared by Aarti's unexpected behavior.

Andy motioned with his hand and asked all to be silent. He called his father and explained the situation.

"I will leave for Pirangut tomorrow evening."

"Just tell this to Aarti, I will put the phone on speaker phone."

"Aarti dikra (child in Gujarathi language). Just don't worry. I will start tomorrow, and the two of you will be married at the first muhurat" (auspicious day).

Aarti started sobbing. "No uncle, they will not let this happen."

"Trust us we will get you married to Andy." Both mother and son said.

"No, No, I will go with Andy." She was crying more loudly now.

His father continued on the phone "Aarti, you have just become afraid. Maaji (mother of Aarti) let her go with Andy. Anyway, they have to live their lives together. I will be there day-after tomorrow with shagun (gifts exchanged on engagement). Let's fix the marriage at the first possible date."

"How can I let her go now? What will people say?"

"She is too afraid now. However, I trust Andy." Then addressing Andy "Andy take good care of her. "And then again, addressing her mother "Maaji, See there is only so much we can do once the children grow up. But you stop worrying now. She is as much our daughter as she is yours. So take the name of god and leave everything to god."

Andy put his mobile is normal mode.

"Thanks papa."

Vishal brought out a box of Peda's (milk sweets distributed on auspicious occasions).

"C'mon, both of you. This is a good occasion. Let us eat some sweets."

No one was really in the mood. They all looked at Aarti, who was mumbling something in-audible. But they accepted the sweets and also gave to Aarti.

"Let's go." Aarti continued.

So Andy looked at Kiran and Mother and sought their permission. They nodded their head.

"OK. Let's go."

Kiran came to drop them to their car. After allowing them to take a lead, he followed them in his car.

All this was happening too soon. Andy had not been ready for this sort of anti climax or new climax situation.

That's what friends are for

Jay had gone several times to the Training room, but all he could get was a few 'Hi's' from Andy. Both Andy and Subba were engrossed in the testing. Subba was very meticulous in the testing and so was Andy. They tested every single routine to perfection. Jay wanted to know what had happened the last evening. Was Aarti OK? So many questions bombarded his mind, but he could not get Andy away for a moment to talk about last evening.

They were very seriously testing the OTS.

The Operator Training Simulator or OTS has become a very key part of chemical process plant operations. The process plants like the PTA plant are run by computer systems called Distributed Control systems or DCS.

The operator sees some pictures of the process and values that tells them the state of the process. To do so, the

DCS is connected to controllers which are themselves computers which do process control functions. And these controllers are connected to devices in the field that tell them the state of the process like temperature, pressure, flow and so on.

These instruments are like the doctor's thermometer, Blood pressure box and stuff like that which tell the patients health status to the doctor.

In petrochemical process plants, these Distributed Control Systems are connected to valves and motors that act to keep the temperature, pressure and flows within limits.

Now operators operate and have to respond to different scenarios of the process plant. The Operator Training Simulator is similar to this Distributed Control System but instead of the actual plant, there is another computer program that mimics an actual plant. The pumps, valves, plant equipment behavior is programmed into its software.

There are many things in the OTS and requires subject matter experts to program it.

The nearest popular equivalent is a flight simulator software. Here you are operating a flight in a virtual environment. The flight simulator could have various airports, landing conditions, landing problems programmed to test piloting skills.

The OTS lets the operator's test various plant conditions and problems that they may encounter and get accustomed to the best response to such adverse events.

The company promised its clients that they had world class training software and a robust training program. Hence, so much effort was put into a mock system. Operators had to operate through the OTS at least 20 hours every quarter, where a minimum 4 hours were tests done by a competent supervisor.

Jay looked at the two, testing the system seriously. He decided to wait till the tests were over. Later Andy ran into Mani and Jay had to wait some more.

Only god knows how testing it is to a friend, to wait for such critical information of their friend's life!

When Andy was done, he wanted to rush home.

Jay wrapped up his activities. Anyway, he had done very little this day. His mind wanted to know what had happened to Aarti and Andy. Hope they had a happy ending . . . or rather a new happy beginning in life . . .

Jay walked the way to the station with Andy.

"So what happened? Everything OK?"

"Yes and No."

"Tell me what happened."

"Nothing big. Her mother and brother had scared her. Told so many things. When I went there, they were not so happy. Then Aarti got very scared, and she was not ready to leave me. Finally, she asked me to apply 'kumkum' to her and said she will come with me."

Andy was wrapping up the events into short sentences. This is not what Jay had expected. Andy used to be such a good story teller. In the past he could describe, holding a girl's hand in a period of half an hour. Explaining each emotion and action and reaction that occurred. How he had approached the act of holding hands, how she had responded, how many times she had retracted her hand and so on. This was so different!

"Andy! The suspense is killing me. So she is in your room. It seems unbelievable, but tell me the details."

"Yes I know, but believe me, I have to rush home. You don't know how many times today, I had thought of running away from Subba, but he wanted to do all these tests. Anyway, in the morning she was alright.

Even her brother came after us.

So don't get any wrong ideas."

"Not like that man. I wanted to know that you were alright." Jay lied.

"Yes. Nothing bad really happened. But her brother contacted someone near college, and they told stories that scared them."

"Yes, your name and reputation sent fear through the hearts of all fathers and brothers with young daughters and sisters in those days."

"I suppose the reputation is difficult to repair."

"As they say 'Badh aacha badnaam bura'"(A saying in Hindi meaning that a bad person fares better than a person with bad reputation.).

"Very true. But then what happened? Were they ready to accept that you have changed."

"They were doubtful, but Aarti did not listen to them."

"What Next?"

"Papa is coming tomorrow morning. Then fix marriage and that's that."

"That calls for a party man!"

"Anytime . . . anytime"

"Shubh kaam mein deri kyun?" (Why delay starting a good activity)

"I have to go home tonight as Kiran and Aarti are waiting. Then a lot of quick planning to do. Plan for my honeymoon and things like that.

"You may not get any leave for your honeymoon. With the issues with the Automator."

"I heard that the MD is not happy over the Automator situation." Andy was happy that the subject shifted to work. There is only so much that you can divulge about your relationship with your wife.

"Yes, even I heard so. There is a big meeting the day after to resolve the same."

"Jay, bear with me. I will fill you in with the details. Just give me a day."

"I will Andy."

"And Jay, you may have to fill in my place, so that I can go to my honeymoon."

"OK. Let's sit tomorrow and plan a handover."

"Thanks"

"That's what friends are for man."

All's well that . . . Unhh
well . . . Ends . . .

<hr>

Everyone was assembled in the conference room. The teleconference call had just started.

"Our MD is very unhappy Marshall." Mani started.

"You could say that again. We have the division head and a set of people from St Louis coming in to analyze the situation. You guys must have applied some heavy pressure."

"Our MD must have. The situation demands this. When we placed the order on you, we never expected to be stuck in this situation.

All your people and yourself too, assured us and me personally that the feed mix Automator was the right solution for PTA44."

"Yes but nobody could have imagined that we would get into this space constraint."

"But we sent your people to the site, and they should have highlighted the space constraint." Ramesh chipped in.

"There were several lacunae in the site. The drawings were not available at that time and they had to make the sketches with their hand and that on a piece of napkin paper. The personnel on the site were very uncooperative." Marshall replied.

"That looks like a simple excuse. The guys were there for three days and should have got this beam in their drawing" Ramesh continued.

"There were many other activities to be done and this was just one of them. They did what best they could do under those circumstances."

"Our contract with you states that, it is your responsibility to have the Automator working. It is your responsibility." Srinivas entered the conversation.

"The contract clearly states that the conditions required for installing the Automator is your responsibility."

This was going in the wrong direction.

"Marshall . . . team . . . we need to let go of the past now and find a solution." Mani intervened. "Our MD and your management are already involved. This failure will be a failure on all of us and will affect all of us. So we need to find a solution.

And that is the reason why this meeting has been called."

Everyone was silent for a few minutes.

"Well, frankly, for the last few days something has been bothering me, but I cannot point my finger and say that's it." Mani had something nagging in the back of his mind for the last few days.

"I will put the drawing of the feedmix area on the Shared meeting Screen."

Once Marshall did that, all of them could see the drawing on their screen's

"Can everyone see the drawing?" Marshall asked.

"Yes we can."

"Now what we have done is make a transparent picture of the automator. I will pull that on the shared meeting screen now.

Can you see it now?"

"Yes."

"I will retrace the step and place it in the original position." Here it fouls with the wall on the right."

"Yes that wall is too close." Mani knew they had been through this earlier.

"After this we changed the orientation to go to the left. This we thought was ok. However, those two beams foul now."

"They put the beams when they changed the size of the feedmix vessel. It was a part of their upgrade program some 15 years back."

"Now we thought of how we could change the design or rather do minor tweaks to fit into this space. NADA. We do not have a way of doing that." Marshall tried to put a tone that said that it was impossible. "We have to redesign and make a new 'Bonsai Automator.'"

Mani then asked each and everyone if they had any ideas.

All answers were negative.

"So that's it, I suppose, unless we come with an idea to reduce the size of the automator itself."

"The design would take a couple of months, and then the fabrication would take two more. All this comes with stopping all work and just doing this design at the innovation center and pushing all jobs back and doing your fabrication. Do we have this kind of time?"

"What will be the cost?"

"I cannot even give you a ballpark figure. This is just a rough idea that we discussed the last couple of days."

"Send me the details and let me take it up with the MD."

So the call was over with no answer to their problem.

"Well that's that. For the last three four days, something about the automator was bothering me. My wife had said that you could solve it like you did during Sundar's party in my home."

"I had just placed the juice container on top of . . . Eureka!" Srinivas chirped.

Mani quickly realized the idea that had struck Srinivas.

"You mean place it one floor up."

Ramesh also realized that this could be feasible. "There are 12 lines, three valves and four flow-meters in that floor. We will have to relocate them." Their experience from actually running such a plant came in handy. Ramesh could visualize the activities to be done.

There was a renewed enthusiasm in the room.

They quickly made sketches and roughly estimated the material that would be required and the time needed to do this activity.

"It would require just one day and that too around 16 hours doing it."

Let's not get over enthusiastic about this. We have to inform the MD and then see what he says.

Mani called the MD.

"Sir, we have figured a way to fix the feedmix automator thing."

"What's the idea?"

"We will place the automator one floor above. There are a number of process pipelines and valves and flowmeters. But that would require some material and activity of around 16 hours to be done."

"Hmnnn . . ." The MD was thinking. "It would require executive approval from the client's board. I actually liked the smaller Automator concept."

"But Marshall said that he would have to prioritize the activity and would cost."

"You have to look at the options, deal with the client and see the best way forward Mani. But the client was very skeptical of making changes to their old design. We have to keep that in mind. So the modifications one floor up may not go through"

"OK sir."

"And Ramesh and Srinivas, train the operators on the new procedure. It has to work for three months.

Good thinking guys.

And anything else?"

"Andy is getting married, next week."

"Why . . . Congratulations Andy."

"Thank you sir."

"OK guys. Have a nice one."

"Same to you sir"

Epilogue

⋅⋅⋙⋘⋅⋅

There are some very important events in an Indian's life. The most important being marriage. Marriage almost rules one's life in India. People spend their whole life, and save everything for this one event called their daughter's marriage. Andy was tied up with so many arrangements that need to be done for this marriage. Andy realized that the marriage industry was bigger than his control system world and industry!

Then you have annual festivals and rituals, often religious. So we can say that religion plays an important role.

And in today's modern life, an event that finds prominence is foreign travel. In older day's there used to be very few who got to travel abroad. Most of these people were laborers and technicians traveling to the Middle East Arab countries. Whatever be their status abroad, they were respected here for their wealth.

Then came the IT revolution and all engineer's looked for that one thing in their resume. Foreign Travel! And nowadays, anyone who has not gone out is looked at with disdain!

"So who have we selected to go to Korea?"

"Ramesh needs to go. He has put in the effort."

"Also send the ethics complaint guy. I want him to know that we hold no grudges."

"OK." Mani had not considered sending Subba.

"Who will cover instrument side?"

"Andy is busy with his marriage. It has to be Jay, his reliever."

"Has the handover happened smoothly?"

"Yes sir."

"Ok, then, let's get the formalities done."

"You have told Andy, that any issues that Jay cannot handle and his honeymoon gets over."

"Yes sir, I have made him responsible and told him the same."

After so many years, the MD felt that he and Mani had started thinking and performing things the same way. Could he move him up the ladder without disturbing the operations? There would be ripples and some issues, but Mani would learn.

Mani called the team in.

"Ramesh, Subba and Jay, as you all know that the Automator is in the critical path. The client management has approved the small Automator change. This is called the "Bonsai Automator" Project.

We need to expedite the delivery.

From 16 weeks we have to come to six weeks.

This challenge is with all of you. Or for all of you to meet"

"Sir, when do we have to travel."

"Next week."

"Sir that is exam time! I cannot go."

"Ramesh your son is in Eighth . . . na."

"Yes sir, but I take his education very seriously." I forgot that more important than marriage is a son's and for some modern parents, their daughter's education. Knowledge has always been respected in this land. Even knowledge for knowledge's sake has been respected. However, now knowledge is 'frenzy'.

There is a race for better grades. The business for better grades is bigger than the marriage business in India.

"Ramesh, I was discussing with the MD a few minutes ago, and I had put forward your name."

"Ramesh he is in 8th yaar (friend) and will manage." Subba intervened.

"Nahi yaar (no friend), he has performed poorly in last semester. With 10th approaching in two years, I cannot risk. These are key years."

"Ramesh, are you sure?" This looks like a good opportunity to let pass."

"Yes. I am confident. Sir, send Srinivas. He is the right candidate for this task. It will require a lot of ideas, and he is the idea guy."

"What an idea sirjee." Subba mocked. ('What an idea sirjee' is a popular one liner of a popular telecom advertisement).

"And Jay, are you geared up for this?"

"Yes sir. I am ready."

So Srinivas, Jay and Subba went on a routine task to crash a project to Korea. And what an adventure it turned out to be. But that's another story.